The Fresh Grave
and Other Ghostly Stories

The Fresh Grave

and Other Ghostly Stories

by Raymond Bial

with illustrations by
Anna Bial

Face to Face Books
Mount Horeb, Wisconsin

Face to Face Books is a national imprint of Midwest Traditions, Inc., a non-profit organization working to help preserve a sense of place and tradition in American life.

For a catalog of books, write:

Face to Face Books / Midwest Traditions
P.O. Box 320
Mount Horeb, Wisconsin 53572 U.S.A.
or call 1-800-736-9189

Library of Congress Cataloging-in-Publication Data

Bial, Raymond.
    The fresh grave and other ghostly stories / by Raymond Bial. — 1st ed.
      p.   cm.
    Summary: A collection of ghost stories in which Hank and his 'fraidy-cat sidekick Clifford explore old buildings and cemeteries around the central midwestern town of Myrtleville.
    ISBN 1–883953–23–5 (hc: alk. paper). — ISBN 1-883953-22-7 (pbk. : alk. paper)
    1. Ghost stories, American.   2. Children's stories, American.
[1. Ghosts—Fiction.   2. Short stories.]   I. Title.
PZ7.B46995Fr 1997
[Fic]—dc21
                                            97-29651
                                          CIP
                                          AC

First Edition
10 9 8 7 6 5 4 3 2 1

For Anna

Table of Contents

Prologue

A Word from the Liars' Bench

You won't find Myrtleville on any map, at least not any that are known to me. Some folks claim our little village is just imaginary and doesn't exist anywhere on the face of the earth. But you seem to have found your way here, so I expect you can look around and judge for yourself how real this place is.

Actually, Myrtleville is pretty much hidden away in the woods and hills, not far from the Wabash River. The Wabash, as you know, crosses Indiana from east to west and then turns south, to join the Ohio River where three states meet— Kentucky, Indiana, and Illinois. Together, the waters flow on to become part of the great Mississippi, near Cairo, Illinois.

Years ago, they used to ship whiskey, molasses, and salt pork downriver on skiffs all the way to New Orleans. But since then, our scrap of geography was bypassed by the railroads, and then by the major highways, so we've pretty much been left alone to make our own way.

As you can see by looking at the rolling hills and deep ravines around you, this land is full of shadows, and it gets more than dark at night. It's been whispered that the countryside is thick with ghosts. Now I don't know if you believe in ghosts or not. Like I've always said, nobody knows for certain if there's an afterlife until you're dead and gone, and not many folks are in a hurry to find out that way.

But I do have a batch of stories for you, and I guess you'd call 'em ghost stories.

All these events happened not long ago, a few years back. They mostly involved a boy named Hank Cantrell, and his sidekick Clifford Hopkins. Now, Hank was a strapping young lad, as able in the woods as a young bear. He's always been good-hearted too, and keenly interested in the history of people and places around here. I expect that's why ghosts seemed to pick him out. What better way to learn about the past and its lessons than to get to know the ghosts who inhabit the landscape?

As for Clifford . . . well, he's always been about a foot shorter than just about everyone else, but he makes up for that by talking big. Then again, sometimes all that talking gets him into trouble. At least, Clifford always seems to be talking Hank into dangerous—and unnecessary—adventures. Fact is, Hank and Clifford don't always get along too well, which I've noticed happens to a lot of best friends who spend so much time together.

Of course, most young folks around here are just naturally curious about our local ghosts, having heard plenty of stories from us old-timers, setting right here in our favorite spots on the liars' bench.

I suppose I should describe our liars' bench. It's not much to look at—it's really just a big, thick board, sagging a little in the middle, and held up on each end by a sturdy packing crate. It's just long enough for two or three of us old-timers, but there's a couple of extra crates lying around for anyone who wants to pull up a seat. Just keep out of the way of our whittling knives. If you sit too close, you'll get your shoes covered with little chips of wood.

And then, every once in a while there's a black comet of tobacco juice one of us aims in the general direction of the gutter. But our aim's pretty good. Generally.

I've always enjoyed young folks. Like yourself. I take a keen interest in any youngster who's willing to take a brief moment out of their busy lives to sit and listen to a good story. I figure it's part of a well-rounded education.

So, if you don't mind being scared a little, sit yourself down while I finish whittling this here ball inside a cage. And listen to what happened to Hank, and Clifford, that I'm fixing to tell you about. Mind you, none of these tales is really too scary—at least not today with the sun shining down on Main Street, just beyond our shady little bench here on the courthouse square.

I'll tell you a story or two. Afterwards, you can decide for yourself whether I've made any of them up.

Or not.

Jarvis Satterly
Senior Whittler-in-Residence
The Liars' Bench
Main Street, Myrtleville

The Fresh Grave

O ut on the side porch, Hank Cantrell was easing back
and forth on the wooden swing in the black of a
moonless June night.

As they did most every evening, frogs chorused down in
the marsh and crickets fiddled in the high grass. The hills
and woods around Hank's farm made the hours after sun-
down absolutely pitch-black, as if the very light had been
swallowed up by the hollows. So he was startled when across
the pasture there flowed a white essence, spiraling like a
whirlpool. At first he thought it was just a wisp of fog easing up from the creek bottom.

A strapping boy with blue eyes and straw-colored hair,
Hank stood up to see better, his hand trembling on the cool
metal of the pump handle. The approaching white fog
might have been a trace of mist, but instead of drifting ran-
domly, it flowed directly toward him. At age fifteen, Hank
knew every rock, fencepost, and tuft of grass in that pasture,
from doing chores and taking care of the livestock, and the
unusual appearance of the mist traveling toward him disturbed him considerably.

He started to retreat into the house where his parents
and brothers and sisters were reading and playing board

1

games in the parlor, but he was so curious, he couldn't take his eyes off the strange mist advancing over their land. Gradually, as he watched, it assumed the shape of a person and he stepped back in shock. Then as it whisked across the strawberry patch right next to the house, the face of a woman emerged from the fog—old and creviced, with keen eyes reflecting light like an animal caught in the headlights of a car. Hank couldn't determine the source of that light, not for the life of him, because it was so dark that the stars seemed to be drowning deep within the sky.

Just as he was about to flee into the house, a voice called to him, "Hank." The sound wafted across the distance that separated them, reaching him in a whisper. "Hank Cantrell, I need you."

The boy's hands shook. He was so frightened that his entire body felt on the verge of breaking apart.

"Come here, Hank," the old lady called from the mist. "I need you."

Hank glanced over his shoulder to the safety of his family. He could run inside, but he kept telling himself, "I know this land. I should be safe on my own farm." Yet as he stepped off the side porch and approached the old lady, he could hardly feel his feet beneath himself. "What am I doing?" he repeatedly asked himself, as if he had lost control over his own actions.

But when he was just yards away from the figure, it spoke again, "It's me, Hank. Hattie Rutledge."

Instantly he recognized old Hattie and, much relieved, said, "You gave me a start, Mrs. Rutledge. I thought—well, uh, never mind. Say, what brings you out tonight?"

Wisps of gray hair floating about her face, she said, "I want to talk with you."

Hank wondered why she was dressed entirely in white, the fabric so delicate that it floated as light as air. Her pale blue eyes had a wild, almost transparent look to them. He glanced back to the porch window from which a comforting light shone and said, "Why sure, Hattie. Mom and Dad will be glad to see you."

"No, out here," she said. "No one must know but you, Hank."

"How come?" Hank wasn't in the habit of keeping secrets from anyone, least of all from his parents.

"No one but you, Hank!" she cried, her eyes flaring with an eerie blue light.

Goosebumps rose on Hank's arms, and he shivered like he was freezing from the inside.

Now, Hattie Rutledge was just about the oldest person in Varnell County, loved and trusted by all, and she knew more about local history than anybody. For many years— as long as Hank had been alive and then some—she had made a study of it, writing articles for the *Myrtleville Weekly Gazette* and even a book which had been published by the Varnell County Historical Society.

Hank was well-acquainted with Hattie and he knew that she could be trusted completely. So he followed her past the strawberry patch and the chicken coop. Just under the basketball hoop on the side of the barn, she paused and told him, "I've got a little job that needs doing, and I'm counting on your help."

"Why is she asking me?" Hank wondered to himself.

Seemingly able to penetrate his thoughts, she explained, "You've always been a boy that folks can count on, Hank. You've always been a hard worker." Aware that he had that reputation, Hank swelled a little with pride, yet for the sake

3

of humility he maintained a sober expression on his face. Hattie went on, "You've always been able to do a good day's work. Well, tonight I've got a good *night's* work for you, if you're willing."

Hank shuffled his feet. "Well, I don't know, Hattie. It's getting awful late."

Hattie pleaded, "It's for a good cause, Hank. And it can't be done without your help."

Anxiously, Hank rubbed his palms on his jean legs. He was scared all right, but offered, "I'm willing to help 'long as it's for a good reason. I know you wouldn't steer me wrong, Hattie."

"You've got to promise never to tell a living soul!"

Although he didn't know why she was asking him to keep a secret, Hank swallowed and told her, "I promise."

"Come on!" Hattie urged, suddenly agitated.

"Where are we going?" Hank thought to ask.

"To Spring Hill Cemetery."

Hank stopped cold. "Just what are we going to do there?"

"I'll explain on the way," she said, taking his arm. Her touch felt light and cool to him. "We've got to get there before it's too late."

They walked along through the dark, down a tractor path that led to a bridge over the creek. There were scattered woods on either side of them, which further obscured the faint light of the stars.

Glancing over her shoulder, as if to make sure no one was eavesdropping on them, Hattie explained, "Lately there have been grave robbers at work in Varnell County."

Hank nodded. He had heard the stories.

"More'n likely they're plain vandals. God knows there's nothing of value to rob hereabouts, especially in graves. People die as they lived—dirt poor. But once they're dead, poor folks have got as much right as anybody to rest in peace. Trouble is those grave robbers are hard to catch. Sheriff Rollins has laid out there more'n one night already trying to catch them, but he usually falls asleep. And those violators are crafty. Likely they've spotted him on those nights and haven't dug up any graves or done any other damage. But old Rolly can't spend every night camped out in the graveyard. So I've got a plan to stop them good, and permanent."

Hank swallowed. "Permanent?"

"Yes, for forever and a day. You said you were willing, didn't you?"

"Well, I . . . uh . . ."

"Then let's hurry!"

"What about my parents? Shouldn't I have told them?" Hank asked, glancing back to his home, the lights of which were fading in the distance.

"Don't worry about them," Hattie said. "They'll think you've gone to bed and won't miss you."

Hank wondered how she could be so certain that his parents would not discover his absence. He wasn't at all sure that he wanted to get mixed up with these violators of the dead, especially as Hattie began to explain her scheme to him, but he had already promised her. It was a little over three miles to Spring Hill Cemetery, that is, if you took a shortcut through the woods and pasture. The old graveyard covered most of a field at the south edge of Myrtleville. Like so many teeth, the tombstones littered the slope at angles, interrupted by clumps of daylilies and oak trees.

"Are you sure this will work?" Hank asked, short of breath, wondering why Hattie wasn't in the least winded by their rapid pace.

"Dead certain."

"Don't say that."

"There's a fresh grave on the slope just waiting. For you, Hank."

For *me*, Hank thought, with a ringing in his ears, because the plan called for him to be buried alive.

Hattie removed a small bag of flour from the pocket of her white dress and used it to powder Hank from head to foot. Then, indicating the open coffin at the bottom of the rectangular hole, she said, "Climb in."

He hesitated. "I'm not so sure I can do this, Hattie. What if you can't get me out in time? There's only so much air in that coffin and—"

"Have faith, boy!"

"But how will you get me out?" Hank asked.

"I won't," Hattie said. "It's the grave robbers who will dig you up."

"What if they don't come?"

"Then I'll dig you out myself."

Hank wasn't so sure. Hattie might be spry, but she was too old to be handling a shovel for any length of time.

"How long will I be buried?" he asked.

"Until they come for you."

"But how long before my air runs out?"

"You'll have a couple of hours or so," she said.

Since he had promised, and since Hattie was a person to be trusted, Hank climbed down into the cold hole and lay down in the pine box. For a second, he caught a glimpse

of the wide-open sky, flecked with stars. Never had he seen a more inviting sight. Then the wooden lid slammed down upon him.

Instantly he was trapped in absolute black.

In panic he tried to push open the coffin, then he beat upon the walls, but shovelsful of damp earth were already thudding down upon the lid, much more quickly than he imagined Hattie could possibly work with a spade. As the earth accumulated over him, the sound gradually softened, coming from a greater and greater distance, and then all was silent.

Hank tore at his hair. He beat and kicked at the coffin walls, and scraped the inner surface until his fingers bled, all the time reproaching himself, "Why? Why? Why did I agree to this crazy plan—to be buried alive! Hattie must have gone mad!" His thoughts swirled in confusion. Then he fainted outright.

It could have been minutes or days before he gradually surfaced to consciousness. His mind was lost in a blur of visions and colorful fragments of dreams, and he was certain that he was asleep at home in bed. Grinning to himself, he sat up—only to knock his head against the lid of the coffin.

"Why?" he demanded of himself. "How could I let myself be buried alive?" Again he vented his terror on the walls, until gradually, in that absolute black, he lapsed into a strange calm.

He wondered if he would have enough air in the narrow box, if he would ever stand on the earth again, if he would ever again behold the sweet light of day. After a while, he simply lay there thinking of nothing, until—

"What was that?" he asked himself, the sound echoing back to him in his confinement.

"It must be my imagination," he told himself. Then he heard it again—a muffled thudding and then a scraping of metal on the wooden lid directly over him. Faintly, he heard laughter, drunken snorts, and a rough voice insisting, "I get to crack this one open, Junior!"

"No, you don't!" another man's voice answered.

"But you got to bust up the last one!"

"Well, you done wrecked two in a row before that!"

"I sure as heck didn't!"

"Okay, we'll all open up it together."

Hank collected himself, lying stiff and wide-eyed as Hattie had instructed. The creaking of the lid as it slowly opened sounded to him like the entire sky wrenching itself apart. In the distance there were brilliant, sudden flashes of heat lightning, but not a sound of thunder, just that anguished creaking sound as the lid was pulled back.

Strangely, Hank felt that he was high up at a great distance, looking downward, and that the sky far below him was nothing but a vast ocean into which he was about to plummet. The wind flashed around him as he slowly sat up, tilting forward, into an immense void. If he kept falling into the deep sky, he would end up orbiting the earth, he thought, always looking downward, without a body or a soul, just himself and the universe around him.

Out of the corners of his unblinking eyes, he saw the utter terror in the faces of three men—the Leach brothers! Usually Orville, Junior, and Ferris Leach hung out at the Sinclair station on the way to Boggsville. They had been a few years ahead of Hank in high school, before they'd dropped out, but they didn't recognize him now, not with the flour dusted all over him.

"It's alive!" Junior gasped.

"No it ain't, it's dead!" Ferris answered.

"Then how come it's movin'?" Orville asked.

"It's a ghost!"

As Hattie had instructed him, Hank raised his hands as if to strangle them and demanded in a deep, formal voice, "Why do you disturb my rest? Can I not rest in peace?"

Their faces twisted, the three guys were already stumbling backward. Junior cried, "We didn't mean nothin'. We was just havin' us some fun. We won't do it again. Not ever again."

Hank sprang out of the coffin and screamed, "If you ever do, I'll bury you alongside of me for all eternity! Do you hear me?" He made like he was going after them, and they ran as if they'd seen death itself—which, in their minds, they most certainly had.

Getting the shakes again, as he recalled his recent burial, Hank scrambled out of the cold hole. From behind a spruce tree, Hattie appeared. She cackled, "It worked! I'd say we cured them once and for all!"

"Do you suppose so?" Hank asked, unable to control his nerves which crackled like electricity through him.

"Yes," she said, looking at him curiously. "I expect that the only thing worse than being dead and buried is to be buried alive. Wouldn't you think so?"

Knowing the feeling all too well, Hank nodded.

"Well, thank you," Hattie said. "I know it was hard for you to lay down there, Hank, probably the hardest thing you've ever done in your young life. But now you know something—more than most folks, old and young alike, and here you're only fifteen."

Hank asked, "You want me to cover up the coffin?"

She looked strangely at him, her blue eyes going soft. Then shaking her head, she said, "No, honey, you've done more'n enough work for one night. What's left to be done, I'll have to do myself."

Hank glanced briefly down at the black rectangular hole, then turned back to her, but Hattie Rutledge had vanished.

That night he walked home, neither scared nor happy, just filled with wonder over the amazing complexity of the universe.

At the hand pump on the back porch, he washed off the flour, at least most of it. Then he quietly entered the house and slipped into his bed, sleeping so long and deep that his mom had to call to him several times before he awoke the next morning.

"Hank, I'm not yelling up these stairs again," she said. "You've got chores to do and here it is practically six o'clock in the morning!"

He bolted upright, dreaming that he was still buried alive, and was thankful to see the light angling in through the window. At first he thought the whole thing had been a dream—until he noticed the flour which remained in the folds of his shirt and jeans. He dressed in clean clothes and went downstairs where his mom asked him, "Are you going to the funeral today?"

"Funeral?"

"Yes. You mean you haven't heard? Old Hattie Rutledge died the day before yesterday."

11

"Day before yesterday? But I just saw her. I . . ."

His mom looked at Hank a moment, then said, "It couldn't have been her, Hank. She's been dead for nearly two days. Now eat your eggs before they get cold."

Hank shook, suddenly chilled to his very bones at the thought that Hattie really had been a ghost.

"Are you all right, Hank?" his father asked, his arms planted firmly on the table.

"Sure," Hank muttered in the general direction of his plate.

"He just doesn't understand much about death," his mom said gently. "He being so young."

But Hank knew something about death, which thereafter gave him a better appreciation of every day of his life. That afternoon, he stood at Hattie's graveside, and found himself looking down into the very same hole he had occupied the previous night.

The Leach brothers were also in attendance. They were shaking like they had a bad case of the chills, and, though Sheriff Rollins could never figure out why, there never was another grave disturbed in all of Varnell County.

The Curse
of Walking Shadow

O ld John Dawson owned one of the largest farms in
Indiana, including an enormous stretch of woods, but
he never lived there. An absentee landlord who lived off in
distant Chicago, he rented the dairy operation to a local
farmer who took care of Dawson's big herd of Holstein cattle as well as several hundred acres of corn and tobacco.

What most interested Hank Cantrell and just about every other boy around was the vast woods at the back of the
farm, because it was the closest thing to wilderness left in
their part of the country. The Dawson woods abounded
with deer, squirrels, raccoon, fox, and even a few coyotes.
At the edge of the stand of oak and hickory trees, coveys of
quail sifted through the brush.

Although Old Man Dawson had posted yellow *Prairie
Farmer No Trespassing* signs all around his land, Hank and
the other boys regularly ignored these warnings as they
climbed the fence and roamed the woods at will. To Hank,
the signs were almost like formal invitations, especially since
he knew that Old Man Dawson never came down from
Chicago where he lived a life of luxury. The man also had

posted *No Hunting* signs, but it wasn't the wildlife he wanted to protect, just his own property.

Nobody ever hunted on that land, however, not because of the signs, but because of the Curse of Walking Shadow.

This practice of community use of the woods went on for years—in fact, for all of Hank's life—until one October day when word went around that Mr. Dawson and his only child, a son whom he absolutely adored, were going to visit the farm, and that they were planning to hunt in the woods.

"What are they going to hunt for?" Hank asked Jarvis Satterly, one of the more distinguished occupants of the liars' bench on the square in Myrtleville.

Mr. Satterly had a pure white beard, and bluish-gray eyes that were so soft they looked like they were about to dissolve into the smoke of his pipe. He knew just about everything about everybody in the county, having lived there for all eighty-odd years of his life. So when Hank asked what the Dawsons were going to hunt, Mr. Satterly answered, "Deer most likely, but knowing John Dawson, he'll shoot at anything that gets in his way. I've run into him a time or two over the years and I tell you, Hank, it's never been a pleasant experience. He's a mean one, pure and simple. You'd be advised to stay away from him. And if you do meet up with him, no matter what you do, don't dare cross him."

"I plan on steering clear of him, and that woods of his, too," Hank assured old Mr. Satterly.

"You be sure to. Dawson is the kind of man who thinks he owns everything, including people. He and that spoiled boy of his have got the disease of *owning*. No matter how much they've got, they have to have more. It's a bad disease, Hank—and most always fatal."

"They don't sound none too friendly," Hank said.

14

Mr. Satterly said, "You just remember what I told you."

Hank thanked him and was turning for home when the old man called after him, "There's no way of knowing for sure, but I believe the Curse of Walking Shadow is real, and I got a feeling Old Man Dawson is gonna come smack up against it, which is another reason to steer clear of him."

Hank planned on following Mr. Satterly's advice. He had plenty of work to do on his family's farm. But come first light that Saturday morning, a brand spanking new jeep tore up the lane to Hank's house. Out of the vehicle stepped none other than John Dawson and his boy, Sonny, both with shotguns cradled in their arms.

Having just finished chores, Hank stood on the back porch by the hand pump staring at them.

A big-bellied man with a bald head, Old Man Dawson was notable for a glass eye, supposedly from an injury received in a fight with one of the workers at his factory in Chicago Heights. His boy, Sonny, was slender by comparison, with callow skin as if he never got any sun, crow-black hair, and a sneer permanently affixed upon his face.

Hank became even more wary with their appearance when the old man called, "We want to talk to Hank Cantrell. That wouldn't be you, would it, boy?"

Hank eased out to the edge of the porch. As much as he hated to, he admitted, "Yeah, that's me, all right."

With his good eye, Old Man Dawson squinted at Hank. "We hear you been trespassing on our land."

Unable to lie, even to the likes of Old Man Dawson, Hank said, "Well, uh . . . that's right."

"Can't you read, boy?" Sonny asked, as if he himself was just about the most important person in the world and Hank wasn't much more than a dumb animal.

Hank stared Old Man Dawson fully in the face, noticing that the glass eye was oddly larger than the real eye. "I've never hurt anything up there. Not a thing."

Old Man Dawson spat onto the ground. "That's for us to decide now, isn't it? Seeing as how I own every square inch of that land."

Hank just stood there, wondering what they were up to. He just couldn't imagine the old man being very riled up about his poking around in those woods every once in a while.

Old Man Dawson heaved a loud sigh. "We sure don't take kindly to trespassers and we were figuring we'd have to call in the law—have them arrest you. That would teach you a lesson now, wouldn't it? That is, if you have any sense to begin with."

Sonny took a step toward Hank and declared, "That's what I wanted to do. Have them put you behind bars, boy!"

Hank went weak in the knees. He'd always abided by the law, except for this innocent trespass, plus he knew he wouldn't be able to stand being cooped up inside a jail cell. It was his nature to be outside on the farm, and roaming the woods and fields thereabouts.

With his single eye, Old Man Dawson looked sweepingly around the Cantrell farm and, in his own sweet time, said, "'Course, we could make us a deal."

Hank began to worry even more now. The word "deal" always sounded a little suspect to him.

"I hear you know all the land hereabouts, like the back of your calloused hand," Old Man Dawson went on. "Well, we're aiming to hunt it and want you to guide us."

"No, sir," Hank said emphatically.

"We'll pay."

16

Although he could see that the man was getting angry, Hank shook his head and said, "Don't want your money."

Locking his single good eye upon him, Old Man Dawson told him, "Get me straight, boy. We're not asking you. We're telling you. You're gonna escort us over every inch of that ground, and do whatever else we tell you to do."

Hank studied the overweight man and his puny son, not liking what he saw. Although Mr. Satterly had told him not to cross Old Man Dawson, Hank wasn't easily bullied. He said, "You can't hunt that land."

Dawson swelled like a giant toad. "Don't you go telling me what I can and can't do. I *own* every leaf and every twig. I can do whatever I want with it."

Hank set his jaw. "Nobody owns that land. It's protected by the Curse of Walking Shadow."

Old Man Dawson flared. "Don't you dare tell me that I don't own that land, boy! Or about any stupid Indian curse, either!"

Sonny laughed. "You ought to just sell the land to that logging company that wrote to you, Daddy. Then folks around here'd know who owned it for sure."

"There is a lot of hardwood up there just going to waste," Old Man Dawson acknowledged.

"It's virgin timber," Hank informed him, knowing from his father that it was one of the last old-growth stands in the area. "You can't touch it."

"Yeah, yeah," Old Man Dawson said impatiently. "Because of the Curse of Walking Tree or some such hooey."

"Walking Shadow," Hank corrected him.

"Whatever. I heard all about it and I don't believe a word of it."

According to Mr. Satterly, years ago, when the Kickapoo Indians had been defeated in a battle with white men on their sacred hunting grounds, just east of Sugar Creek, a young warrior had risen up and placed a curse on the land. "He was a slight youth who moved in absolute silence," said Mr. Satterly. "On his face, he carried the grief of an entire race. He'd gone East to study the white man's ways, not to be like him, but to better understand how to live peaceably with him. A peace-loving man, when it became obvious that the Kickapoo were going to be killed or driven from their ancestral lands, Walking Shadow declared to the whites, 'You have the power, this day, over our land. But what is just and right abides through the seasons. We have lived and thrived here, not by weapons but through our knowledge of the land and its spirits. As you deprive us of our hunting ground, so shall you also be denied its abundance. I curse this land now and for as long as the white man shall try to rule over it.'"

At first nobody believed the Curse of Walking Shadow. But whenever they shot at a deer or rabbit in those woods, even at close range, the white hunters either missed or the animal vanished into its own tracks. Or if it appeared that a hunter had killed an animal, upon their approach the animal would spring to its feet and flee, unharmed.

Like the Indian tribes themselves, over the years the teeming, abundant wildlife was systematically exterminated across the length and breadth of the region, except for this last forgotten patch of wilderness along the Wabash River.

At one time the Erie Canal ran diagonally through Indiana, following the river to connect with the Ohio and the

Mississippi. The trade route went from upstate New York all the way to New Orleans, the flatboats carrying hog bellies, whiskey, and corn. It appeared that the Wabash Valley would become a central trade route, that is, until the railroads redirected traffic. Then the region was pretty much forgotten, and nobody knew the story of the Curse of Walking Shadow except for the scattered farmers and people in Myrtleville.

Out of respect, Hank, like his neighbors, never hunted that ground. He tried to honor the land as had the Indians, for Hank knew that land truly belonged to no one; that, on the contrary, people belonged to the land.

Old Mr. Satterly had also told him and whomever else would listen that Walking Shadow had been mortally wounded that day by a white man's bullet. In the mist of the battlefield, his spirit had risen into the air, declaring, "One day long into the future, a white man will return to this place, speaking loudly of his dominion over the earth. Upon this man, I shall place a curse far worse than death."

Hank could imagine nothing worse than death, and he didn't want to have anything to do with Dawson, lest he be caught up in the curse.

Yet the old man bawled, "Let's go, boy!"

Not having much choice, Hank reluctantly went along with Old Man Dawson and Sonny. They drove down Greenfield Slab for a few miles, then turned up a rutted farm lane between the woods and a cornfield. When they got out to walk, Hank led them deep into the woods. He did his best to make as much noise as he could, hoping to protect the wildlife he loved, but the deer were so abundant they appeared around practically every bend in the trail.

The old man and his son shot again and again, with no luck.

"I'm sure I got that one doe," said Sonny, puzzled. "Right between the eyes."

"We got to get closer!" Old Man Dawson yelled. He was so frustrated and angry that he struck at Hank with the butt of his gun.

Sonny just laughed when Hank ducked away from the blow, jeering, "You stupid hayseed."

Thereafter, trying to stay on the man's blind side, Hank led them into thickets of blackberries and across patches of low ground where the father and son sank to their knees in the muck.

"Hey, what the hell do you think you're doing?" Dawson demanded, as he tried to wrench his legs out of the mud.

"You got to watch your step," Hank told him.

Old Man Dawson and Sonny observed that Hank sure knew where to place his feet on the soft ground of the marsh and hadn't so much as gotten his toes wet.

"You think you're so smart," Sonny remarked.

Hank told them, "You wanted me to lead you to the wildlife."

Afraid to push his luck, Hank guided them along a deer trail. Increasingly red-faced, Old Man Dawson and Sonny shot again and again, at every bird and animal that came within their sights—squirrels, blue jays, chipmunks, and even woodpeckers. The discharge of their guns resounded through the woods all that day.

Along about five o'clock, Hank said quietly, "I told you that you couldn't hunt this ground."

"Why you!" Old Dawson whirled around furiously, his face swollen and purple, pointing the gun directly at Hank's chest. "One more word out of you and I'll blow you and your big mouth to kingdom come!"

Hank stood paralyzed.

"Hey, why don't we hunt *him?*" Sonny said, his eyes bright, his face twisted.

At first Hank thought that he was joking, until Dawson squinted down his gunsights at him and demanded bitterly, "Think we'll miss if we shoot you, boy? Think you'll fall dead if we blow a hole clear through you? Or do you think you're protected like your damned Indian and his curse?"

Hank was sickened by both of them. They were so bent on killing something, anything. It was as if they couldn't tolerate the life abounding around them.

Just as the old man lowered his gun, saying, "He ain't worth the trouble," Sonny poked the cold steel end of his gun into Hank's chest and said, "We could make out like it was an accident, Daddy. Nobody'd know but us."

Old Man Dawson got a soft, peculiar look on the face, and Hank realized just how much he had spoiled his son— to the point where he would allow the boy to do anything, even take the life of another person. What kind of strange love was this, he wondered, in which a man poisoned both himself and his child?

Hank's only advantage was that he was smarter than both of them put together. He glanced swiftly up a tree, as if he'd spotted a hawk or some other wild bird. As Old Man Dawson and Sonny followed his line of sight, Hank made a break for it.

"There he goes!" Sonny cried. "Come back here, or I'll shoot!"

"Go ahead and shoot," Old Man Dawson yelled, as if Hank's act of defiance entitled them to fire away.

Behind Hank the guns discharged, the blasts tearing through the leaves and branches over his head and all around him. The lead slugs whizzed past him, dangerously close.

"He's getting away, Daddy," Sonny whined.

"Well, go after him!"

They tried to keep up with Hank but didn't stand a chance, for Hank was lean and strong and knew the woods well. Panting, Sonny consoled himself by saying, "Look at the scaredy-cat run!"

Old Man Dawson shouted, "He's about as brave as that Indian."

Laughing, Sonny said to his father, "I got a better idea, Daddy. It's just about dark. We can shine deer!"

Besides being illegal, to shine a flashlight in the eyes of a deer so that the animal stood blinded, paralyzed by the glare, was not a fair way to hunt, but Hank realized now that they were both mad.

Once out of range, Hank turned back to circle the old man and his son, stalking them in the gloom. Unarmed, he didn't know what he'd be able to do, but he worried that the Indian's curse might not work at night, and he wanted to make sure the Dawsons killed no deer.

Before long, walking deeper into the woods, the darkness growing thick around them, the father and son soon froze a deer in the conical beam of their flashlight. With eyes like liquid silver, the deer stood perfectly still.

"Let me have first shot, please, Daddy."

Old Man Dawson licked his lips greedily. "Well, all right. Just so's I get my shots too."

As Sonny raised the gun to his shoulder and sighted the deer, Hank sprang forward. He meant to push the barrel aside, but the gun discharged and the slug tore through Hank's shoulder. "Dang, I missed!" Sonny cried. In the dark, gripped by their obsession, neither the father nor the son noticed that they had shot Hank. Pressing his hand against his shoulder to slow the flow of warm sticky blood, Hank crawled into the bushes as Sonny shot again. The deer jerked, its eyes rolled backward, its legs buckled, and it crumpled to the ground.

"You got it!" Old Man Dawson cried. "We're gonna need a truck to carry out all the game we shoot tonight!"

However, as they approached the deer—it vanished, as had the other game that day. In its place, there gradually appeared a frail Indian in buckskin clothes and moccasins, with intense black eyes.

The Indian pointed at Old Man Dawson and said slowly, ominously, "Henceforward you will wish you were dead, so strong is the curse I now place upon you."

"You can't threaten me!" roared Old Man Dawson. "You don't know who I am. I'm John Dawson. I *own* this land."

"From this day forward it is the land which will own you."

"The hell you say!"

John Dawson raised his gun toward the Indian, except that in the dark and in the confusion, the gun was pointed directly at his son. Raising his hands in front of him, Sonny backed up, crying, "Daddy! Don't shoot me!" But it was too late. The blast knocked the boy backward, a hole blown into his chest.

"Sonny! Sonny boy!" Old Man Dawson cried. "My God! What have I done?"

As the man crouched over the dead body of his son, he begged Walking Shadow, "Bring him back. Bring him back!

You have the power! You bring back all these stupid animals. Raise up my son!"

The Indian shook his head. "I only have the power to do what is right. If he is ever to come back, you will have to be the one to make it happen."

"I'll pay!" cried Old Man Dawson. "I've got enough money to buy this woods a hundred times over. I'll turn it into a park. That way nobody will be able to hurt anything here."

"This land is already protected—by a power beyond your money," the Indian told him.

Old Man Dawson shook the lifeless body of his son. He tore at his own hair. He sobbed, "Sonny boy!" Finally in desperation he pointed the gun at himself. He pulled the trigger. Click, click. He reloaded the gun, but still it wouldn't fire.

"You cannot kill yourself," Walking Shadow told him calmly. "I will not permit you to follow the path of the coward."

"But I can't stand it! I'll give you anything—my own life—anything. Just return my son to me."

The Indian shook his head. "This is your curse. Many generations of my people were sacrificed at the altar of the white man's greed, and now you are condemned to remain here forever, grieving for your child."

"But I can't stand it!" Old Man Dawson cried again. "He was my only child! I can't stand it."

"Daddy," a voice called. "Daddy, help me!"

"Sonny! Thank God, you're back. Where are you, son?"

Gradually the body of Sonny Dawson vanished. "I'm over here, Daddy," the voice called. "Help me, Daddy."

"Where are you, Sonny?"

"Here, Daddy. Please help me."

Old Man Dawson turned to Walking Shadow. "Where is my son?"

"That is for you to find out on your own."

The voice of Sonny called out, now from the bushes, now from the trees, and now from the path, but try as he might, Old Man Dawson could not locate his son and bring him back from the spirit world. He thrashed through the brambles, and sank in mud, and ran into trees in his frantic search, but it was to no avail.

Hank never fully understood the power of that curse until years later when he had his own children, and found out how precious they were to him, more so than his own life.

Alone, Hank limped home that night, and Doc Patterson patched up his shoulder. Being young, he mended quickly. He might have believed that it all really had been a dream, but, like the aching scar on his left shoulder, the memory of it stayed with him for the rest of his life.

Old Man Dawson disappeared. People said that he fled the area to avoid being prosecuted for shooting Hank and for murdering his son, although the boy's body was never found. Only Hank knows that the old man is still out there somewhere, hunting for his lost son.

On occasion, you can see his footprints in the sand along a lonely creek bed. Or you can hear him calling to the night sky like a wolf, trying to swallow back his grief like so many splintered stars.

And some nights when you go out into the woods, you'll see an eye peering from behind a tree. It could be an owl or a deer, but then again it may be the old man with one glass eye, forever searching for his lost son.

The Black Hand

Toward the end of June, Hank went on a camp-out at a nearby state park with his 4-H club. He enjoyed the thick woods which blanketed the park with shade, as well as the clear water of Sugar Creek and the winding trails through the ravines. That night, after a long day of hiking and exploring, Mr. Satterly, a local farmer and their leader on the camp-out, said to them, "What say we tell a few ghost stories before we call it a night, boys?"

Having grilled hot dogs and toasted marshmallows, the boys were seated around the campfire, its orange light flickering over their young faces.

One by one, the boys told their favorite ghost stories, passed down through generations of Myrtleville farmers. Hank thought some of the stories were interesting because of what they revealed of each family, while others were frightening, and he would have enjoyed them all more, except that after every one, Rodney Bressler cried, "Awww, that wasn't scary!" or "Come on, that was boring."

Rodney was a plump boy with small gray eyes like BBs sunk into the folds around his cheeks and brow. His father had a dairy farm just up the Greenfield Slab from the Cantrells' place, so Hank knew him pretty well, but he had

27

never liked the boy, partly because of Rodney's excessive appetite. Also, the Bresslers acted as if they were better than other people, bragging about their new ranch home with all its modern conveniences. "Gadgets," Mr. Satterly called them.

What Hank most disliked about them was that they readily asked others to help them out with baling hay and harvesting crops, but were seldom willing to lend a hand in return when their neighbors needed assistance. Just that spring, when Joseph Taswell was laid up with a broken leg, every farmer in the area had helped to plant his corn, except the Bresslers. Last autumn, when Willard Shuck had a heart attack and was in the hospital, every farmer in the area showed up to bring in his crop, except the Bresslers.

When he wasn't criticizing the ghost stories, Rodney was either picking his nose or making low animal noises to himself. Finally Mr. Satterly said, "Aren't you a little too old to be acting this way, Rodney?"

Rodney blinked twice. "Me?"

"Yes, you!"

"These stories are just plain stupid," said Rodney in defense of himself. His comment riled the other boys, including Hank, because many of their stories were part of each family's history.

Mr. Satterly swelled up. "And I suppose you think you can do better?"

Rodney lifted his nose a notch higher and said, "Any day of the week."

"How about today?" suggested Otis Livingston, a short boy with bright orange hair and an abundance of freckles. "Right this very minute."

"Go ahead, Rodney," Mr. Satterly said. "Be our guest."

Rodney immediately got flustered. "Well . . . well, I could if I wanted to."

"He could, except he can't think of one!" cried Otis, rocking back on the log, his auburn eyes flickering in the light of the campfire. "Him with his big mouth and little brain. He can't come up with even one story!"

The other boys teased Rodney for a while, until he declared, "I could tell all kinds of stories, except there's no point to it. None of these stories is true and besides—"

"Mine's true," objected Otis.

"And so's mine," added Hank, who had told them a story about the first funeral wake his grandfather had attended.

In a clamor all the boys claimed the truthfulness of their yarns.

"Well, I don't believe none of it," Rodney asserted, folding his arms and frowning deeply. "There ain't no such thing as ghosts and all that supernatural nonsense, not in this whole entire world."

Mr. Satterly was looking intently at him. "I wouldn't be so sure of that, Rodney," he said.

"You mean you believe in ghosts?" Rodney scoffed. "You're a grown man! How can you believe in that hocus-pocus?"

"I'm not saying that I do or that I don't," Mr. Satterly said gravely. "I expect the only way we'll know for certain is when we're dead and gone, and I don't know anyone who's in much of a hurry to up and die. The only thing I'm pretty sure of is that people don't know hardly as much as they think they do. Fact is, people who are absolutely sure of everything usually end up being wrong."

"Well, I don't believe in any of that supernatural stuff," Rodney bragged.

All of the other boys were pretty much fed up with him for ruining the campfire stories, and now for creating a scene. Earlier that summer, Hank might also have doubted the existence of ghosts, but not after coming face to face with the ghosts of Hattie Rutledge and Walking Shadow. But that evening, it didn't matter so much whether the stories were true or not, just that they were having a good time and learning more about each other.

Fiddling with a twig, Mr. Satterly studied Rodney a while, as if he were trying to figure him out. Then he said, "We'll have just one more story tonight before we sack out, and I'm the one who's going to tell it." He squinted at Rodney. "And for your information, boy, this story is true."

Rodney snorted, "Sure it is."

Ignoring him, Mr. Satterly began, "You know, many generations ago this land belonged to the Piankeshaw Indian Nation." Hank leaned back and imagined natives paddling their canoes down Sugar Creek, then climbing the rock bluffs to trot in absolute silence along paths through the dark, green woods. Mr. Satterly explained, "However, one by one, the Indian tribes were defeated and forced to sign papers giving their land to the white men.

"Only one Indian chief, named Little Hawk, whose hunting territory was right around here, refused to sign the papers, even after several defeats at the hands of the white men. The army captain who finally captured Little Hawk wanted to kill him, but seeing that the Indian would rather accept death than betray himself, his people, and his land, the captain hesitated. Besides, if he killed the Indian, the treaty paper would still be unsigned.

"'What shall we do?' the captain asked his lieutenant, who was second in command of the army regiment.

"The lieutenant, who was a cruel man, thought a while, then said, 'Cut off his hand, hold the fingers around a pen, and make the signature for him. Then it will be official. We can honestly say that it was signed by the hand of Little Hawk. Then leave the Indian to die, since he longs for death, and we will have no witnesses to challenge our statements.'

"The two men laughed at the cruel trick. They untied Little Hawk and, with soldiers holding each of his legs and arms, they lay his right arm across a stump. With an ax, they cut off his right hand at the wrist. But Little Hawk refused to cry out, even though the pain obviously must have been terrible.

"Tying him back to a tree, they left the Indian war chief there to slowly bleed to death. The captain took the hand with its bloody stump, formed the fingers around a quill pen, and scratched out the name 'Little Hawk' on the papers. The captain and lieutenant then signed their names as witnesses that it was written by the hand of Little Hawk, which it was in fact, though not in spirit.

"The evil deed happened in these very woods," Mr. Satterly emphasized, making a sweep of his arm to indicate the black darkness that pressed to the edge of their campfire. "Strangely, when the soldiers went back to Little Hawk to show him the paper with his signature and to make fun of him, he was gone! They supposed that other Indians in his tribe had crept out of the woods and rescued him, but no one ever knew for sure.

"The captain then made a terrible mistake—he threw the severed hand of Little Hawk into the weeds, as if it were

31

of no more value than a piece of spoiled meat. You boys work with your hands just like the Indians. So you know what I mean. Not only had the soldiers defiled the name of Little Hawk, but they showed little respect for that which had made him an able man."

The boys sat there staring into the fire, all of them except Rodney who scoffed, "Oh, that ain't nothin' but make-believe!"

Hank was furious that Rodney had again broken the spell of the story. It may or may not have been historically accurate, but in the ways that mattered, it seemed true to him, because what had happened to the natives was, in most cases, worse.

Mr. Satterly went on, "Legend has it that the hand is still out there, with a life of its own, trying to be reunited with the body and soul of Little Hawk. But it will never find peace, because we have damaged the land hereabouts so much."

"That ain't true!" Rodney muttered under his breath.

"Oh, shut up!" said Lyle Wright, a wiry boy with hair as black as crow feathers.

Frowning at Rodney, Mr. Satterly said, "There are those who claim to have seen the ghost of Little Hawk. And it's harmed more than one person. In fact, people in these woods have disappeared altogether, never to be seen again."

Rodney snorted his disbelief.

However, the effect of the story upon the other boys was so great that they just stared at old Mr. Satterly, the story-teller, with their mouths hanging slightly open, their faces embraced by the orange glow of the campfire.

"Now, what say we get us some rest," suggested Mr. Satterly, glancing darkly at Rodney. "We've had a long hard day of hiking, and it's past midnight already." Although they'd planned on staying up all night, the boys were exhausted from their day of hiking, and no one really complained.

The light from the moon and stars could barely penetrate the canopy of trees, so the woods were tremendously dark—so dark they could scarcely see their hands in front of their faces, let alone find their way to their tents.

No one was particularly anxious to sleep in the same tent with Rodney, because he was still making fun of everything and because he kept moaning, "Oooooooo," and making other stupid noises just to annoy the others and keep them awake. Hank, Otis, and Lyle, who had been assigned to that tent, were just managing to get to sleep when Rodney got hungry. Although they'd had a huge dinner, he began to munch potato chips and other junk food, which he'd brought in his duffel bag. Not once did he offer to share with the others, even if they had been hungry. He just kept noisily eating away and tossing the empty bags out of the tent.

Finally, the other boys in his tent began to drift off to sleep, in spite of Rodney's moaning, "Ooooooooooo, I'm gonna get you!" and the loud crunch of his potato chips.

Hank was just nodding off himself when he saw a sight that made his blood run ice cold—a glowing black hand, crawling slowly like a spider toward their tent! As it drew nearer, he saw that it had a bright red stump where it had been chopped from the wrist. The rest of the hand had turned black and shone like neon, with a dark purplish light the color of a bruise.

Hank didn't dare utter a word, let alone wake up any of the others.

Still stuffing junk food into his mouth, Rodney was oblivious to the hand, until it reached the triangular opening to the tent where it rose into the air and hovered near his face.

Hank could see the terror in Rodney's beady eyes, but the boy managed to compose himself and say, "Come on, you guys. I know it's just a trick. You can't fool me!" He swatted at the hand with his pillow, but it deftly veered away from the blow.

An instant later the hand flew at him, clenching his throat. Gagging, Rodney thrashed around trying to pry the fingers loose.

Huddled in their sleeping bags, not bothering to look up, the other guys called to Rodney. "Cut it out!" groaned Lyle. "It's late. We've had enough of your dumb practical jokes!"

"Quit clowning around!" Otis said. "Let us get some sleep, will you!"

Only Hank watched as the hand yanked Rodney out of the tent, carrying him aloft, his arms and legs flailing. Crawling out of the tent, Hank rubbed his eyes to make sure that he wasn't dreaming—that it was really happening— then he stumbled after Rodney. He looked on as the struggling boy was borne by the flying hand through the woods, across Sugar Creek, and dumped on a high bluff overlooking the water.

Sputtering desperately to get his breath, Rodney scrambled to get as far as possible away from the black hand, which was again hovering in front of him. Whenever he tried to make a break for it, the hand zipped in front of him. Finally he broke down and whined, "Leave me alone! Please, please, leave me alone! I ain't done nothin' to you!"

Although terrified by the appearance of the black hand, Hank crept forward across the suspension bridge that spanned the deep gorge of Sugar Creek to see if he might help Rodney. Everything around him was absolutely dark, except for the glowing purplish-black light given off by the severed hand.

"What do you want?" Rodney whimpered.

As if in answer, quick as light, the hand threw the boy against a crooked tree growing out of a rock, and wrapped several lengths of rope around him.

"I didn't do nothin'!" Rodney cried.

Out of thin air, the hand produced a small ax.

"No!" shrieked Rodney. "No!"

Without a word, the black hand hacked off the boy's right hand with the ax. Rodney stared in shock at his own severed hand as it thudded to the ground, then at the gory stump at his wrist from which blood was spurting in rhythm with his heartbeat. "No! No!" he moaned as the black hand snatched up his hand and threw it deep into the woods.

"Now you know," a voice said, echoing like thunder from high above the trees.

"Know what?" asked Rodney stupidly.

"You know what it feels like to be treated brutally as we were once treated."

Leaving Rodney tied to the tree, the hand veered high into the sky. "Wait, wait!" the boy called after it. "What about me? What about my hand? I'm bleeding to death."

"Find it, if you can," the voice called.

The black hand then swept directly over Hank, and the voice said, "Return to your teepee. And say nothing of this to anyone."

"What about Rodney?" Hank asked anxiously.

"He is mine," the voice resounded. "You can do nothing to help him. Your friend will be safe. Trust me. But you must say nothing of this incident. Promise that you will remain silent forever!"

Not knowing what Little Hawk was up to, but somehow trusting him, Hank said without hesitation, "I promise."

"Now go!" the Indian demanded.

Wide-eyed, Hank did as he was instructed, but he didn't sleep a wink that night. Sitting in the triangular-shaped doorway of the tent, he watched for Rodney. Occasionally, when the wind veered in his direction, it seemed to carry the moans of the boy to him. Time and again he was tempted to creep out to help the boy, but something deep inside told him that he must trust the black hand.

The next morning as they crawled out of their tents, yawning and rubbing their eyes, the boys began to ask, "Where's Rodney? What's up? Where's that dope off to now?"

Hank sat bolt upright. Briefly, he had drifted off, and for a moment he'd thought it had all been a dream—but Rodney was gone.

"That joker!" said Otis, shaking his head. "He's just trying to fool us into thinking something happened to him!"

Saying nothing about the black hand, lest he further endanger Rodney, Hank led a search party to the bluff, hoping to rescue the boy, but he had vanished. There was not a trace of blood or any other evidence of a struggle.

All that morning the boys looked for Rodney, with no success. Hank could see that Mr. Satterly was both worried and angry. Grinding his teeth, the man said, "If that boy is playing some fool joke on us, I'll tan his sorry hide."

Hank was tempted to tell him about the black hand, but thought that he should wait until they were well away from those haunted woods.

By mid-morning, they were all getting very frightened and Mr. Satterly was about to call the sheriff when Rodney stumbled out of the woods, dirty, scratched, and wide-eyed. Hank noticed immediately that his hand had somehow been reattached to his arm without the slightest scar.

"Where on earth have you been?" Mr. Satterly demanded.

Barely able to talk, Rodney quivered, "It got me last night. It carried me off and . . ."

"What carried you off, Rodney? Your imagination?" demanded Mr. Satterly. "You should know better than to wander off from camp. We've been looking all over for you. We just about called the police. That was a very foolish prank."

"But it took me!" Rodney cried.

"What did?" asked Lyle, scarcely believing him.

"The Black Hand!"

Everybody laughed.

"Quit trying to fool us," Otis said. "You got lost in the woods. You're just looking for an excuse."

"No! No! It's true! The Black Hand snatched me up and flew me through the air. Then it tied me to a tree, and cut off my hand!" He raised his right hand to show them.

"Your hand looks all right to me," Mr. Satterly noted.

"That's because Little Hawk put it back. I met him in the woods. He came and untied me. He's a ghost, and he is real! He said he cut off my hand so I'd understand his pain. But he said if he didn't restore my hand, he wouldn't be any better than those soldiers who cut off *his* hand."

Shaking their heads, everybody just looked at each other.

Otis said, "You should've told that story last night, Rodney, when you had your chance. It's a pretty good one, even if it is a whopper."

"But it's true! You got to believe me!"

"You just got lost on your way to the latrine," Otis claimed again. "Admit it, Rodney."

"Probably fell in," Lyle suggested. "I bet you he's been down at Sugar Creek all this time, trying to wash off."

Nobody ever did believe the boy, except for Hank, who had witnessed the whole incident. Everybody talked about the time Rodney Bressler had gotten lost in the woods, and had a good laugh at his expense. Still, they could never quite explain why Rodney thereafter became a more agreeable boy. They also were surprised when, unlike his father, Rodney was always willing to help out his neighbors when they needed him—although he often complained of a slight pain in his right wrist.

Haunted Barn

The barn stood upon a rise with not a single tree around it, which made it loom, gray and foreboding, in the soft prairie sky. By any measure it was huge—four times the size of most other barns. Its beams were hand-hewn and a cupola graced its angled roof. Built over a century ago, it had stalls for horses and cattle, as well as an immense loft, divided by upright timbers. What was most unique about the structure, however, was the number of rooms for storing grain and farm equipment, including harnesses and saddles. People said it would have been the perfect place to play hide and seek. That is, if it weren't inhabited by a fearsome ghost.

On the occasions when he and the other boys were hired to unload hay at the barn, Hank Cantrell liked to climb the board ladder in the center of the structure, straight up, nearly a hundred feet to the cupola. If you were brave enough, you could climb out the window and, clinging to the sill with the very tips of your fingers, edge your way around to the nearly level peak of the roof. One slip and you would fall to your death. Despite—or perhaps because of—the danger, Hank and some of the other guys often climbed to the roof where they could take in a breathtaking view of the surrounding woods and fields, the Wabash River shimmering in the distance.

Clyde Purcell owned the barn and all the land around it, in addition to his own farm, although the old house had burned down years ago. The corn crib, chicken coop, and other outbuildings had long since disappeared as well. Clyde used the barn for storing hay, nothing more, and absolutely no one dared go up there at night, because of the voice.

One evening in September, just after they'd started back to school, Hank Cantrell, Rosie Morgan, Clifford Hopkins, and some other kids were gathered around Mr. Satterly on the liars' bench in Myrtleville, talking about the barn. The old man shook his head and admitted, "I'm dead certain that barn is haunted. But I don't know how or why it came to be that way."

"Well, maybe we'll just have to go over there and find out," declared Clifford, swelling up like a bullfrog. Since Clifford was just about the biggest coward in the county, the other kids simply snorted at him.

"You're scared of your own shadow," scoffed Otis Livingston.

Nobody believed Clifford would go up there at night, at least not without Hank. Although very different in manner and appearance, the two boys had been best friends all their lives. Clifford's blond hair was as curly as lamb's wool and he lent new meaning to the word skinny, whereas Hank had always been as strong as a young bull. And while Clifford fancied himself a worldly young man, Hank was as rooted to his family's farm as an oak tree.

Just as Clifford admired Hank's strength and ability, Hank envied Clifford's way with members of the opposite sex. Clifford could talk constantly, never saying anything, but thoroughly amusing the girls in their freshman class. The two boys had always gotten along, until last spring when they'd both gotten interested in the same slender green-eyed girl, Rosie Morgan.

Despite Clifford's persistent attempts to impress her, Rosie had thus far spent her time ignoring both boys. For his part, Hank was so shy that he'd yet to begin his campaign for Rosie's heart. Yet this evening he felt obliged to challenge his friend Clifford's claims, telling him, "Nobody's going up there, especially you, Clifford. You're just bragging."

Clifford spat through the gap between his two front teeth, a talent he'd used to impress kids across the county, and said, "You just watch me. I ain't scared of nothin'."

"Now you hold your horses there!" Mr. Satterly called after him as Clifford turned down the street with a flourish surely meant to impress everybody. "I don't know if that's such a good idea."

"Why not?" asked Clifford, turning back toward the group.

Although each and every person standing there knew the story practically by heart, they weren't near tired of hearing it. Mr. Satterly reminded them, "You know how strange sounds echo through that barn, like it's a huge cave, even if it's filled up with hay? Every night that voice calls, 'Let me out! Let me out!'"

Otis nodded. "I heard it myself once."

Spitting into the gray dust at his feet, Mr. Satterly remarked, "Is that a fact now?"

"Yeah, I really did," Otis went on. "Once we were late getting a wagon of hay unloaded. The sun was just melting away, and me and Les Walker were working as fast as we could. Right at dusk, we were hightailing it out of there when we heard the voice calling, 'Let me out.' It sounded so desperate and lonesome and sad."

Some nights, Hank and Clifford, with other friends of theirs, had crept as close as they dared to the barn to listen for the voice. With the wind coursing through the grass, it was hard to distinguish sounds, but they always thought they heard it.

"What do you think it is?" Clifford asked, acting as if he were not in the least disturbed by the story. Yet Hank knew his skinny, curly-haired friend would be terrified of a leaf if it happened to fall too close to him.

"Well, I don't rightly know," said Mr. Satterly. "But I think it's connected with the burning of the farmhouse, way back at the turn of the century. They had a beautiful white clapboard house with a wrap-around front porch, and all this frilly gingerbread trimwork under the eaves. The style was called Victorian, I believe. It even had a turret like a castle. It was a rare sight in this part of the country. When I was a boy I used to drive by it with my folks just to look at it. Well, one night, after a big family fight, it burnt down. That's what I heard anyhow.

"A family named the Jordans lived there and they were real secretive people. First the mother run off—some say all the way to Oregon—leaving the father, who everybody called Jumbo, and his daughter. Now Jumbo was a huge man, like a wrestler. He could lift a hundred-pound bag of feed in each arm, and tote them bags around all day like they were feather pillows. He only bothered to shave when he thought about it; which wasn't often. Otherwise he was well-kempt, with the blackest hair.

"His daughter had the same black hair, but she was slender and as pretty as a dogwood blossom. Most every young man in the county had his eye on her, except that Jumbo scared them all off. Big and powerful as he was, he was still a decent sort except when it came to her. He was so jealous about his daughter that it pretty near drove all three of them crazy. Not long after the wife ran off, the house burnt to the ground. And the girl fled, too, followed by Jumbo himself who sold what was left of the place, including the barn, for half what it was worth."

"But what about the barn?" Clifford asked. "How come it's haunted?"

Mr. Satterly shook his head. "Nobody knows exactly how that barn came to be haunted. There are those who think a terrible crime was committed there, but no one knows for sure, since no one ever heard from the mother or the daughter again. We heard Jumbo went after them, but never did catch up with them. He worked on a barge hauling corn and whiskey down the Mississippi River for years. He never was able to settle down again, and he died a sad and bitter man. That's all I know."

"Seems like after all these years, someone would have found out why the barn is haunted," ventured Hank, glancing at Rosie out of the corner of his eye.

Mr. Satterly shook his head. "No, son. And you want to know why? Nobody's been fool enough to stay up there long enough to find out."

As Mr. Satterly talked, Clifford paced back and forth, becoming increasingly agitated. Finally he cried out, "What do you mean 'fool enough'? It takes guts to go up there. That's what it takes!"

"A body would have to be crazy to go inside that barn at night," said Otis. "What if that ghost got ahold of you?"

"I ain't scared of no ghost!" Clifford said.

"Sure you're not," scoffed Russell Hendricks.

"Maybe I'll just go up there right now!" Clifford declared. "Any of you other guys want to come with me? What about you, Hank?"

Scowling, Hank glared darkly at his big-mouthed friend.

"You mean you'd go up there at night?" asked Mary Ethel Freeny, looking admiringly at him.

Clifford swelled like a bantam rooster. "Sure as shootin'. We'll go up there tonight, right this minute! Won't we, Hank?"

The last place on earth Hank wanted to go was to the haunted barn, and he hated being a show-off, but he could hardly back down now, not in front of everybody, especially Rosie. He wished she would give some indication whether she liked him or not, but she just stared at Hank and Clifford as if she couldn't make up her mind.

"Come on," urged Clifford.

Reluctantly, Hank accompanied his friend to his old Chevrolet pickup.

"Been nice knowing you!" Otis called after them.

Mr. Satterly yelled, "You boys be careful now! It could be dangerous in there!"

As they drove through the dark countryside, Hank didn't say a word to his friend until they pulled into the old farmyard and turned off the headlights. Drawing a long sigh, Hank studied the huge gray barn and said, "You and your big mouth, Clifford. Look what you got us into."

"There's nothing to worry about," said Clifford.

"What do you mean?"

Clifford smirked. "Do you really think there's a ghost in there?"

"Well, I don't know. There could be."

"There's no ghost in that barn," Clifford assured him.

"How do you know that, for sure?"

"'Cuz there ain't no such thing as ghosts. Come on, I'll show you."

Hank had yet to tell Clifford of his previous encounters with the supernatural earlier in the summer for fear that his friend wouldn't believe him. He watched as Clifford got out of the pickup and strode confidently to the barn. Turning back he called, "Come on, Hank. Hurry up."

Reluctantly, Hank followed his friend, just as the wind gradually picked up, and the large double doors on the barn began to creak back and forth.

"See," said Clifford, as they paused directly in front of the looming black square of the doorway. "I don't hear anything. There ain't a thing to be scared of. It's just the wind."

"Let's go home then," suggested Hank.

"But we got to go inside," Clifford insisted. "To prove there's no ghost."

"After you," said Hank.

"Well, all right, but I'm going to tell Rosie that it was me who went in first, and that you were scared just being here."

"It's not that I'm scared. I've just got sense enough not to go messing around where I don't belong."

Just as Clifford started toward the door, a soft voice called through the wind. Clifford braked to a stop. "What was that?" he asked.

"What do you think it was?" Hank said.

Faintly, as if it were coming from a great distance, they heard it call again, "Let me out. Please let me out."

Suddenly Clifford was backing away from the barn.

"What's the matter?" asked Hank. "I thought you were so brave and all. I thought you wanted to go first."

"Well, we came here and heard it," Clifford said. "Now let's get the heck out of here!"

Hank grabbed Clifford by the arm as the skinny teenager started to run back to the pickup. "I thought you wanted to find out about the ghost."

"We can tell people we went inside."

"That would be lying."

"Who'd ever know, 'cept us?"

"That wouldn't be right. Besides, we haven't found out what it is, or why it's calling out to us."

Clifford licked his lips. "Well, you go first then."

"Why should I go first when you're the one who was bragging about how brave you are?"

"Because you're bigger'n me."

"You're just chicken," Hank said.

"I am not."

Hank had been hanging out with Clifford long enough to know that they would stand there arguing all night. Finally, he sighed. "All right. I'll go first, but you got to come in right behind me, you hear?"

"Sure, Hank. Whatever you say."

Cautiously, Hank stepped into the black interior of the barn. Several feet inside, he turned around and realized that Clifford was not with him. "Come on. What are you waiting for?"

Standing outside in the white light of the rising moon, Clifford said, "You're doing just fine without me."

"You're scared."

"I am not. One of us needs to stay out here and be a lookout."

"Well then, I'm getting out of here!" Hank said. "I didn't even want to come here in the first place."

No sooner were the words out of his mouth than he clearly heard the voice again. "Let me out! Please . . . I beg you. Don't go. Let me out!"

Clifford's eyes shone as big as pie tins, just as the double doors of the barn snapped shut in a gust of wind, leaving Hank trapped inside the barn. In terror, Hank slammed against the door, but it was latched tight—on the outside. "Unlock the door!" he yelled at Clifford, but received no answer. "Clifford? Are you out there?" Still getting no answer, he squinted through a crack between two planks. His friend was stumbling back down the slope. "Don't you run off!" Hank yelled after him. "You come back here and open this barn door!"

"I can't!" Clifford whined. "I'm too scared."

"But you got to get me out! Let me out!" Hank cried, shocked at how much he sounded like the voice. "Please, Clifford. Let me out."

Clifford crept forward and made a half-hearted effort to unlatch the door and reported, "It's stuck, Hank."

"Try harder."

"I can't get it. It's wedged tighter'n can be."

"Let me out."

Instantly Clifford backed off again, saying, "There it was again. Did you hear it, Hank?"

"That was me," Hank said. "Get me out of here!"

48

Clifford whimpered, "I'm sorry, Hank. I'm just too scared. It's gonna get you, Hank. It's gonna kill you, I just know it." He stood there trembling visibly, then announced, "Hey, I know what I'll do. I'll go get help. That's what I'll do. You just wait right there, Hank."

"You coward!" Hank hollered after him. "Don't you run off on me! You hear me, Clifford!" But it was too late. Jumping into the pickup, Clifford tore off into the night, just as the voice inside the barn called again, "Let me out."

Spinning around, Hank asked the dark interior, "What do you want with me?" Chills swam through him as he realized that he was addressing a ghost.

At first there was no answer, then the voice said, "To save yourself, you must also rescue me."

Groping through the dark, with cobwebs catching at his face, he tried every door and window in the barn, both on the ground level and up in the second-floor loft, but they were all locked tight.

"Let . . . me . . . out." The voice called in desperate pain.

Finally Hank climbed slowly, hand over hand, up the ladder, high in the barn to the cupola. There, the window was not locked and he edged out onto the roof, but there was no way to escape other than to throw himself to his death. As much as he hated to leave the fresh air and moonlight on the roof, he knew he had to go back into the barn, and find the source of the voice. What would happen, he wondered, if he found it, and was able to let it out? Maybe it intended to kill him. Perhaps it wanted to make him take its place as the next captive of the barn.

Clifford will be back soon with help, Hank kept telling himself as he climbed back into the barn. But then, what if nobody could get the doors open? And what if Clifford never came back, which, knowing Clifford, was a distinct possibility. Gradually, as time went by and no help arrived, Hank concluded that something had happened to his friend.

Increasingly desperate, the voice called, "Let me out! Let me out!"

"Who are you?" Hank asked.

The ghost only answered, "Unless you let me out, you'll die here, too."

A great wind filled the interior of the barn, although not a single object moved. It was so dark that Hank could hardly see at all. He felt something touch his shoulder. Whirling around, he lashed out in terror, but it was only an old plow harness hanging on the wall.

On the edge of panic, Hank proceeded to look for the source of the voice. He opened doors to grain bins, and stuck his head into the dark interiors, but had no success. He did come across an old-fashioned kerosene lantern tucked in a corner of a wall, with a few ancient blue-tipped matches.

He tried the matches, which must have been decades old. To his relief, the matches and the lantern worked just fine. Now he had a flickering sphere of light and he could see—except that the light also cast huge, terrible shadows every which way he turned.

"Let . . . me . . . out!"

"What will you do," Hank asked, swallowing hard, "when I find you?"

A howling laugh resounded off the walls of the barn, mocking Hank it seemed. The last thing on earth he wanted to do was to go looking for a ghost, but figuring he had no other choice, he crept forward. "I'll find it, let it out, and then make a break for it," he told himself.

However, finding the source of the voice proved difficult. Although it repeatedly called out to him, the sounds echoed off the walls so that the voice seemed to be coming from several directions at once. Through the long night Hank methodically searched every nook and crevice, both downstairs and in the loft. The barn was suffocatingly hot, so that his jeans and workshirt were drenched with sweat. Hour after hour, he searched, finally concluding that the voice was coming from the first floor.

Downstairs, he again searched every stall, every grain bin, the tack room, the workshop—each and every little room. "Where are you?" he asked, utterly frustrated.

The voice only answered, "Let me out."

Hank was about to give up, when he remembered how people sometimes listened for an approaching train by placing an ear against the railroad track. Pressing his ear against a thick, hand-hewn timber, he felt the faintest vibration each time the voice called, "Let me out." Moving from one timber to another, he concluded that the ghost was in the very wood of the barn. How could he release its spirit unless he tore down the structure, board by board?

He moved closer to what he believed was the source of the voice. Soon, he reached a corner next to the tack room where saddles, bridles, and harnesses had once been kept, and more clearly than ever heard the voice call to him in deepening anguish, "Let me out!" Then—he heard a faint, yet desperate scratching on the other side of the wall.

At first Hank thought the ghost resided in the actual wood planks, but upon closer inspection he realized that a second, false wall had been constructed to form a tiny hidden room, which apparently had been nailed shut many years ago.

"Let me out! Let me out! Let me out!" the voice cried urgently. Now, not just the wall, but the entire barn shuddered to its stone foundation with the fury of its trapped resident.

"Will you hurt me?" Hank asked.

The ghost only demanded, "Let me out!"

Sweating profusely, uncertain of what he was doing, Hank found an iron bar in the tack room, and pried at the boards, wakening the gray dust of the ages. "Let me out! Let me out! LET ME OUT!" the voice shrieked, and there was a mad beating on the other side of the wall.

The wall was tightly put together with square nails, but Hank eventually managed to wrench a section loose. Putting down the bar, he gripped the boards with both hands and pulled with all his might. "Let me out! Let me out! LET ME OUT!" As he tore the wall open, a violent gust of stagnant air rushed over Hank. To his horror, he found himself standing face to face with a skeleton, dressed in old-fashioned clothes, with hands raised, the bones of the fingers like the small, fragile legs of gleaming white spiders.

He noticed that the inside of the wall was scarred with claw marks and covered with dried blood that had apparently dripped long ago from the fingers of the prisoner. Then suddenly the skeleton fell upon Hank, knocking him down and overturning the lantern. There was that mad laughing again, and a whooshing sound throughout the barn, whereupon every door and window in the barn snapped open, admitting a brisk, but soothing wind.

On his back, Hank struggled with the skeleton but couldn't get it off of him until, like a slowly rising mist, a nearly transparent image of a farm boy rose from it. He's my age, Hank thought, although he's wearing old-time clothes. The expression on the ghostly boy's face gradually turned from horror to a wistful smile, then the farm boy ran for all he was worth through the open door of the barn, crying, "I'm free! I'm free! I'm free!"

Hank scrambled out from under the lifeless skeleton, which still remained on top of him, and was heading for the door himself, when he noticed a yellow page fluttering at his feet.

Picking up the page, he studied the scratchy, misspelled handwriting in reddish-brown ink, and read, "This is my story truly told for it is writ with my own blood, and a splinter from the wood of my prison. I know now that Jumbo who nailed me in this wall meens more than just to teech me a lesson. He plans for me to dye here. He goes about his chores whisling, as if I do not exist. When I call out to him, when I beg for water, for mersy, he just goes on melking the cow and acts like he don't heer me. But he does, and I think he injoys my suffring. If not, why would he not have killed me mersyfully when he caught me in the loft with his dotter Betsy? And why does he linger here, after she run off, excep to injoy my pain. His heart is surely as black as his hair.

"Yesterday he spoke through the wall to me, saying that once I'd dyed and the stench of my body had faded he would sell the farm, and leeve to find his wife and dotter. No one but me and him would ever know my fate, and I would be condemed heer in these walls for all eternity. That

53

is what troubles me mostly. I am sure to dye, but must somehow be freed from this place, or forever suffer his injustis.

"To whoever finds me I leeve this message so that you will know my suffring. To whoever saves me I will also give a reward. By all the powers of heaven and earth, I promis that you will find the true love that were denied me."

Stumbling out of the barn, Hank breathed the sweet dawn air, which smelled of timothy and clover. He was thrilled that he had freed the spirit of the imprisoned farm boy, and he was left with a deeper appreciation of each and every precious breath of his own life.

Later that morning, the sheriff identified the boy from the contents of his thin, worn wallet as Les Billings, the fifteen-year-old son of a local farmer. Les had disappeared nearly a hundred years ago. It was presumed that he had run off to Chicago or some other big city.

That evening on the square, the kids gathered around Mr. Satterly to discuss the amazing events of the previous night. Hank had assumed that he would be considered a bit of a hero, except that Clifford bragged, "See, we finally solved the mystery of the haunted barn, and you all got me to thank for it."

"You?" Hank asked incredulously.

"Yeah, if we hadn't gone there, we never would have found the ghost."

"What do you mean 'we'?"

"Well, we both ought to get credit, even though I had to make you go up there. You were scared. Remember?"

"But you ran off!" Hank cried.

Clifford shook his head. "I only went to get help."

"Then how come you didn't come back?"

"I came back."

"Yeah, the next morning!"

Clifford's face assumed an expression of complete innocence. "Well, what else was I supposed to do? I didn't want to wake anyone up in the middle of the night, and besides I figured we'd be able to see better in the daylight."

Hank took a step toward his friend. "What you mean is that you were scared stiff. That's what you mean!"

"Why don't we just forget it," Clifford advised. "I'd say I've got more important things to do." He turned to Rosie and asked right in front of everybody, "How 'bout going for a cherry Coke over to the drugstore with me?"

Studying her feet, Rosie blushed. "Oh, I don't know. I'm pretty busy right now."

"What do you mean? You're just standin' here like the rest of us."

She just shrugged and squirmed.

Already furious with Clifford for lying about the events of the previous night, Hank turned to Rosie and blurted, "Hey, Rosie, why don't you and me go for a walk?"

Immediately, the girl brightened and said, "Sure."

"Hey, I thought you said you were busy!" Clifford protested.

"Well, I guess I am now," Rosie said, her eyes aglitter as she looked at Hank.

"You done a good job last night, Hank," Mr. Satterly called out after the boy as he walked off with Rosie.

"Thanks," Hank said back over his shoulder. As he walked along beside Rosie, he still was not exactly sure what he should say to her. He just hoped for the true love which the ghost of the farm boy had promised him, and in the meantime, he slipped his hand in Rosie's.

Night of
the Dancing Graves

"**B**ut we just got to go out there!" Clifford Hopkins insisted as he was sitting with Hank on the liars' bench in front of Tremont's Drugstore and Fountain in Myrtleville. "There's a full moon tonight. You know what that means? There will be skeletons dancing all over that ol' graveyard!"

Setting his jaw, Hank told him, "We don't *got* to do anything."

"You're just chicken."

"Darn right I am."

The two boys were talking about Barton Hill, an old graveyard overgrown with weeds and daylilies. Occupying a wooded knob at a crossing of two dirt roads, the graveyard was known only to the people who lived in that region. Rumor had it that on nights of the full moon in October, the earth shook and the graves opened, and wooden coffins gradually surfaced. The lids of these slowly creaked open, and ghosts rose from the skeletons inside and danced by the milky light.

"Oh, come on!" Clifford wheedled. "Let's go."

Hank shook his head.

"I don't know why you're always so stubborn."

"I'll tell you why!" Hank said, the heat rising in him. "It's because I know exactly what will happen if we go up there. The first little thing—like a twig snapping—will spook you, and you'll turn tail and run. You'll leave me there, like you do every time we do anything that's the least little bit dangerous."

"No, I won't. I promise. Not this time I won't."

Hank eyed him darkly. "You did this summer when we went up to the Jordan farm."

Clifford licked his lips. "Tell you what. If I do run off on you, I'll give you that new calf of mine."

Hank raised an eyebrow. "The Jersey heifer?"

"Sure enough."

"You must want to go up there awful bad."

"I do," admitted Clifford. "I surely do."

"Why?"

"I just do."

Hank knew Clifford well enough to realize that there had to be something behind his friend's plan. "Well, all right," he said. "You put up the calf *and* tell me why you have to go up to the Barton Hill graveyard so bad, then I'll go up along with you."

"It's a deal." Clifford licked his lips. "Promise you won't laugh."

"I'll try not to."

"I got to impress Mary Ethel Freeny. You see, I kind of like her and, well, they were razzing me up at the cafe today, and I swore I'd go up on Barton Hill just to show them and Mary Ethel that I ain't a coward."

"So you want me to go along to hold your hand so you won't be scared?"

Clifford reared up. "I could go myself, any day of the week! But, well, it would be more fun if we both went, wouldn't it?"

Hank didn't believe him for a minute, but he sure could use a calf, since he and his dad were trying to build a small dairy herd. He said, "All right, I'll go, but if you chicken out on me . . ."

"Thanks, buddy."

"And don't go callin' me 'buddy'."

The two boys got up and headed to Hank's pickup. On the way Clifford cleared his throat and suggested, "Just one more thing, Hank."

Hank stopped on the sidewalk and glared at his friend.

Clifford licked his lips and said, "It's okay if you come along with me, except you don't exactly have to tell anybody you did. I'd sort of like for people to think I went up there all alone."

Hank told himself that he should have known as much. "Well, all right, I won't say anything, but if you run off on me . . ."

"Have I ever let you down before?"

"Not more'n fifty or a hundred times—and that's only in the past year or so."

Against his better judgment, Hank climbed into his old Chevrolet pickup and, as the sun set, the two boys drove the winding backroads to the graveyard. Despite the full moon, it seemed particularly dark out there as they drove into the mild hills, the leaves black against the sky. They arrived at the cemetery to find old cedars swaying slightly side to side, groaning in the light autumn wind. The top of the hill was fairly littered with white stones gleaming in the moonlight.

Hank turned his old truck up the double ruts of the steep lane that led up the hill and ended in a clearing.

Scrambling out of the pickup, Clifford whispered, "Come on!"

"Isn't this far enough?" asked Hank. "Let's just wait in the truck. We can see well enough from here."

"But I need to bring back proof."

"Proof? Like what?"

"I don't know. I haven't thought that far ahead yet. Hey, I know! I'll pick some of them daylilies. That ought to be proof enough."

"That's no proof," Hank contended, since the orange trumpets of the daylilies jammed practically every road shoulder between there and Veedersburg. "You can get daylilies just about anywhere around here, night or day."

Clifford frowned. "You're right." Suddenly he lit up like a jack o' lantern. "I know what I can bring back—a bone!"

"Bone?"

"Yeah, from one of the skeletons. Maybe a leg bone, or maybe even a skull!"

"You can't do that!"

"Well, let's at least get out and see what's there."

"I suppose," Hank mumbled, reluctantly climbing out of the pickup.

As the two boys proceeded into the graveyard, finding themselves surrounded by the chalky white stones, Clifford said, "See, Hank, there ain't nothin' to be scared of."

"Nothin's happened yet," Hank pointed out.

"You wait and see. We'll come out of this just fine."

As they wandered among the gravestones, the black leaves swishing around them, they frequently glanced over their shoulders. Hank whispered, "I just know a ghost is going to jump us. Here we are at the top of the hill. Can't we go back now? You can tell everybody you came here in the deep of the night, and you won't be lying."

"Come on, there's no ghosts going to rise up here, not really. You don't believe any of those old rumors, do you?"

Hank stopped cold. "You don't know the history of this graveyard, do you?"

"Not hardly."

Hank swallowed. "I hear that all the people buried here are from the old Findley Settlement."

"The old Findley Settlement? So? That was over a hundred years ago. Way before the Civil War."

"Well, the way Mr. Satterly tells it, those folks kept to themselves entirely. They had their own community, like the Shakers, or the folks down at New Harmony, only here in the Findley Settlement there were said to be strange things going on."

"Like what?"

Hank shrugged. "Nobody knows for certain what. But there was some kind of terrible injustice, and folks figure that's why the dead in this graveyard are so restless."

Clifford grinned. "Maybe we'll find out tonight."

"I sure hope not. Let's just pick your flowers or something, and get out of here."

"But we got to have better proof than that. You said so yourself."

Hank sighed. "I don't know why I let you get me mixed up in all your cock-eyed schemes."

Not an instant later the wind rose, streaming through their hair and the low grasses around the white stones. The tops of the trees rocked back and forth.

"I feel it!" Clifford cried.

"Feel what?"

"The earth shook!"

"No, it didn't. That was just the wind."

"It did, too!"

"Looks like a storm is coming up. We'd better get a move on before we really catch it. Clifford?" Hank glanced to his left, but his friend had vanished. "Clifford?" At first Hank thought that the spirits had captured his friend, until he glanced back down the slope to see Clifford racing toward the pickup. "Don't you dare leave without me!" Hank yelled.

Abruptly the hill shuddered again, knocking Hank clean off his feet. He tried to get up, but each time he was thrown down again. "Don't leave!" he shouted to Clifford.

His friend was already in the pickup, grinding the gears, and backing down the rest of the hill.

"Hey, you come back here. That's my pickup!"

"I'm going to get help!" Clifford yelled back to him. He glanced just once back at Hank, his eyes large and white with terror before disappearing in a cloud of dust.

Hank cried, "I knew it. I just knew it."

Once again he tried to regain his feet, but another shudder set him down on his backside. "Gosh darn it," he mumbled. Suddenly the hill rumbled like it was going to explode, and each of the graves yawned open.

Hank couldn't believe his eyes.

Ever so slowly, each of the coffins rose to the surface, one by one, and the lids creaked open. Out of them danced a hundred ghosts dressed in old-time clothes. The men had on overalls and blue workshirts, and wide-brimmed straw hats. The women either wore gingham or plain patterns of home-spun cloth, their hair drawn up primly in scarves. They danced about in time to a strange music which seemed to be carried on the wind.

Hank bolted toward an iron fence which bordered the hill, but rising from a grave next to him, a ghost snatched him by the ankle.

"Off so soon?" it asked, its glistening white teeth forming a leering grin. "The dance has just begun."

A ghost in overalls jumped on a wide stump, danced a little jig, and snatched a fiddle right out of the vivid night air. Pairing off, the ghosts danced arm in arm. Hank blinked his eyes again and again, then he slapped himself, but he didn't come awake.

The ghosts cavorted in time with the music, "Flies in the buttermilk, two by two. . . ." They danced around Hank, as if he weren't there, then they snatched at him, howling with joy, as if they'd never known such wild release.

Hank tried again and again to escape, but the ghosts had encircled him, gradually backing him up to the very top of the hill. Suddenly, he tripped and plunged into the black mouth of an open grave.

Desperately, he clutched at the moist earth and the tufts of grass around the lip of the grave, pulling himself up out of the ground.

"Be careful," the voice of a young woman urged him. "It is dangerous for you to be here." He had never before heard such a soft, melodic sound, and he searched the wispy ghosts for the source of it. Gradually, a ghost without a partner, dressed in a calico dress, emerged from the jumble of cavorting figures. As it faced Hank, its perfect teeth worked mistily into what Hank concluded must be a smile.

"Isn't it beautiful?" the ghost asked in the most seductive voice.

"What?" he asked carefully.

"Sweet music carried on the night air."

Before his very eyes, the ghost was transformed into a lovely young woman, about his own age. She had honey-colored hair, and eyes of a violet hue. Hank watched as each of the ghosts gradually assumed flesh, becoming robust men and women with flushed faces and wide smiles. In the plain styling of their old clothes they resembled Old Order Amish, except that many of the women's dresses were patterned.

"Isn't it beautiful?" the woman repeated, catching his attention. "The night. The fresh autumn air. It's so wonderful to be free!"

"Free?" Hank asked, noticing that the people all seemed to be overcome with joy.

"Won't you dance with me?" the woman asked, glancing away and blushing slightly. "I don't seem to have a partner."

Hank could not imagine dancing with a dead girl who moments earlier had been a ghost. He feared that if he touched her, he would instantly be swallowed up in the earth from which she had just emerged. But she was so alluring, so mesmerizing, that he found himself stepping forward to take her hand.

His attraction to the young woman seemed to whip the other ghost dancers into a frenzy.

"Look at Sally Ann!" cackled an old man with loose skin like turkey wattles on his neck. "She's finally happy."

A pudgy old lady shook her head. "All these years without a partner. What a shame."

Breathlessly, Hank reached out to take her hand, and was within inches of touching the white tips of her graceful fingers, when a bolt of lightning crackled across the sky, once, and then again and again.

Gasping and cringing, the bodies of all the people lit up and they trembled as if electricity ran through them. "Stop, you animals!" a powerful voice resounded through the trees, shaking the gravestones to their bases. Atop the largest stone materialized a man dressed entirely in black, clasping a Bible to his chest. Thrusting a crooked finger toward Hank, he demanded, "How dare you tempt that child!"

The man wore a black hat with a wide brim which cast a shadow diagonally across his face, out of which gleamed a pair of fierce eyes. He had a large, curved nose, and his lips twisted into an acidic smile.

"She doesn't belong to you," the old woman gasped.

"Cease your chatter!" he thundered.

"But she doesn't, although you tried to keep her all to yourself in your house."

"I said cease this chatter! I am your leader. I brought you here. We built a perfect community, a utopia in the wilderness. Why should you persist in complaining? You always had food and lodging."

"Utopia?" an old man snorted. "We were no more than bees in the hives. We were slaves to your orders, Montrose!"

"How dare you speak against me!"

"You promised happiness, Montrose, and we found only

empty words. We gave up all of our possessions and traveled to this wilderness with you, yet in all the years we lived here, we were not allowed to ever speak to outsiders."

Montrose jabbed his finger skyward and sparks of blue electricity crackled from its tip. "That would have brought destruction upon us."

The old woman rubbed her hands together anxiously. "We only wanted simple human joys—to love our children, to laugh, to dance."

"Look at yourselves," Montrose roared, "in your clothes of many colors. You should all be wearing black as I commanded!"

"But now we are happy, as we would have been in life if you had allowed us to be."

"You would have lost your immortal souls!"

An old man with flashing eyes pointed at the leader as if he were stabbing him with a knife. "It was you who destroyed us. You imposed such a terrible isolation upon us. We died miserable, each and every one of us—especially Sally Ann, for she had no one other than yourself."

"And now I am taking her back with me!" Montrose announced bitterly. "We'll leave you to your wild and sinful dances. Come here, Sally Ann."

The girl hung her head.

"I said to come here, Sally Ann. I command you."

"Stay with us," the people urged.

A tear slipped down Sally Ann's cheek. "I can't."

"Yes, you can. He's not really your husband, and you owe him no allegiance. He took you to be his young bride, but he never married you. He's just an angry old man. You belong with us."

"But if I stay, I still have no partner. I will remain odd Sally Ann."

"What about him?" the pudgy woman pointed to Hank. "He could be her partner."

Immediately, Hank backed away. Even his Rosie was not as lovely as Sally Ann, but this girl had been a ghost just moments ago. She's dead, he kept telling himself, and if he danced with her, wouldn't he have to join her in the grave at the conclusion of the festivities on this October night?

Hank wiped his clammy hands on his jeans and cleared his throat. Then, looking directly into Sally Ann's eyes, he said, "I'd sure like to, but it's late, and I've got to get home."

"Coward!" hissed the pudgy woman.

"But if you stay," said the man with the turkey wattles, "your action will free us forever from the threats of Montrose."

Montrose appeared to have been absorbed into the depths of his black clothes so that only his pale hands and face stood out against the night. He rocked back and laughed so hard that Hank could see the gold in his teeth. "Yes, go ahead, boy, stay and see yourself buried along with the rest of them, for they are surely doomed!"

"He's lying!" the man with turkey wattles cried. "Nothing will happen to you."

Sally Ann anxiously twisted her hands together, begging him with her big sweet eyes.

Hank swallowed.

"Not sure?" Montrose asked. "Then run away. You won't be hurt, if you simply run. You can be certain of that. No matter what they say, they cannot stop you."

"Is that right?" Hank asked the old man with the white beard.

The old man hung his head. "Yes, you do not have to help us. No harm will come to you, if you choose to leave us."

Hank looked over the crowd of people, all of them robust and attractive, especially when compared to the gnarled figure of the man in black. Yet he recalled how earlier in the evening they had risen as skeletons, with dirt clogging their eye sockets.

He considered his options for only a moment, then resolutely he stepped up to Sally Ann. Overhead the lightning crackled. "Better not!" Montrose shrieked. "You'll be struck dead!"

Hank hesitated.

He bowed to Sally Ann, offered his hand, and asked, "May I have this dance?"

The trace of a smile edged up the corners of her mouth and she said, "Certainly." She was as lovely as an April day, yet the moment she took Hank's hand, the sky whitened with lightning. "Do not be afraid," she said. "We must all die."

"But not now," whispered Hank.

She smiled wanly.

There was a great turmoil in the skies, the black and purple clouds twisting as if in deep anguish. Then, before Hank's eyes, Montrose was abruptly yanked upward into the sky, his arms and legs flailing. When he was nearly out of sight, he shattered in an explosion of light, and his dust was quickly dispersed by the winds high in the upper atmosphere.

"He's gone!" cried the man with turkey wattles. "Your defiance has finally sent him into oblivion!"

Hank simply stood there, the grave people dancing with joy around him. "Come dance with us," they cried in unison. Cautiously, Hank placed his arm around Sally Ann.

That night they whirled around and around. Hank was so thrilled that he scarcely wondered what would happen to him.

Toward dawn, Sally Ann gripped his arm and said, "Alas, I must return to the grave."

Jolted back to reality, Hank asked, "The grave? But if you're free, can't you stay here with me?"

"I am of another century, my love," she said, brushing the tips of her fingers delicately across his cheek. "But at last we will rest in peace. If you wish you may come with me. To the grave."

Hank started.

"Do not be afraid, my love," Sally Ann said soothingly. "You have nothing to fear of the afterlife. I promise you that we will have many happy times together."

Slowly, Hank shook his head.

"I understand," she said, gently blowing him a kiss, as she receded into the night. "Just promise me one thing."

"I'll try," Hank said, swallowing hard.

"Promise that you'll never forget the night you danced with a young lady from deep in the past."

Hank smiled broadly. "I sure won't ever forget you or this night."

As the first streaks of light seeped in at the bottom edge of the eastern sky, the people gradually resumed the forms of ghosts.

"Don't look at me!" Sally Ann cried urgently as she floated back into the grave.

Hank glanced away, so that he would always remember her as a lovely young woman. When he turned back, the morning light was streaming through the trees, and the graveyard was as before—serene and well-kept. An unbroken carpet of grass covered Barton Hill, and one would never have imagined the revelry of the previous night.

Exhausted, Hank walked down the hill to the crossing of dirt roads. As he turned toward home, he saw Clifford approaching in his pickup. Pulling up next to Hank, his friend asked anxiously, "Where you been?"

"What do you mean where have I been? Where have *you* been?" Hank demanded.

"Where do you think? I been right here keeping watch."

"No, you haven't."

"Well, I went for help."

"Sure, you did. Where is the help then? And what took you so long to come back?"

"It was dark. How do you expect me to help you when I couldn't see three feet in front of myself?"

"You owe me one Jersey calf," Hank said, grinding his teeth. He got into his truck, making Clifford move over to the passenger side, and roared down the dirt road.

"Well?" Clifford asked.

"Well what?"

"What happened?"

By rights, Hank should have been furious with Clifford, but if his friend hadn't talked him into coming to Barton Hill and then run off, Hank might never have danced with Sally Ann. Certainly, the night had had its dangers, but he had never known such loveliness before. He considered telling Clifford about Sally Ann and what had happened—for about two seconds—then he answered, "Nothing."

"What do you mean nothing?"

"Just what I said—nothing."

Clifford eyed him. Hank knew that his friend didn't believe him, but to tell him anything would be like having it published in the *Myrtleville Weekly Gazette*. Clifford said, "Come on, let's go down to the cafe for some breakfast. Rosie and Mary Ethel are waiting there. They've been worried sick about you."

Hungry as a bear, Hank drove with his friend to the cafe where Rosie made a big fuss over him, which he appreciated. But then Clifford laughed, "He just got lost up there last night."

"I did not!"

Hank decided to tell the three of them the entire story, except that he didn't think Rosie would really want to hear about Sally Ann. He described the graves opening, the people dancing through the night, and the shattering of Montrose. Clifford smirked and said, "I don't believe a word of it. How 'bout you guys?" Rosie and Mary Ethel just looked at Hank. "It's like I told you," Clifford went on. "Hank got scared and run off. I been looking for him all night."

Hank reared up. "That's not true, not by a mile. If you want to know the truth I'll tell you exactly what happened, and exactly what Clifford did!"

Opening up the menu, Clifford said, "I think the girls have heard enough. Let's just get us something to eat and forget the whole thing."

Ghost Lady

O ne gray afternoon in April, Hank and some other kids were gathered around Mr. Satterly at the liars' bench down in Myrtleville. The old man was just beginning a story, one of his first that spring. But since milking time was approaching and a storm appeared to be gathering in the distance, Hank rose from the bench and said, "I'm sorry, but I got to be going."

"You're not taking the shortcut, are you?" asked Clifford Hopkins, his eyes as wide and bright as silver dollars. "Dark as it's getting today, that ol' ghost lady might get you. I hear she's been out lately."

Hank, whose pickup truck had broken down, responded, "Long as I got to walk home, I'm gonna take the shortcut. No sense in going all the way around just because of some spook house. It's daylight yet, so I don't figure I have much to worry about."

"That ghost lady'll come flying out of that house and get you for sure!" Clifford warned.

Hank knew how dangerous the old gray Whittaker house was supposed to be. Its black windows stared right back at you, and strange noises often issued from the house, like someone was laughing and crying all at the same time.

At night a candle shone from an upstairs window, behind which appeared the blackened silhouette of an old lady who seemed to be peering deeply into the woods and fields around the house. The ghost lady moaned incessantly, "Come home, my boy. Come back to me." Over the years, curious teenagers occasionally had disappeared in the vicinity of the old house, never to be seen or heard from again.

Yet, as he headed for home, Hank said to Clifford, "It's not like it's night or anything. There's no ghost lady going to come out until it's good and dark."

Throughout this discussion, Mr. Satterly had sat quietly, but as Hank departed, he said to him, "You're best advised to be careful, son. That ghost lady, as they call her, is one powerful spirit."

Hank halted right there on the sidewalk and asked, "What's she doing up there anyway?"

Leaning back on the bench, Mr. Satterly drew on his pipe and sighed. "The way I heard it, the old lady's son, Cyrus Whittaker, run off and joined the Union Army, years back in the Civil War. He was her only child and the old lady doted on him until he was practically suffocated. He weren't but fifteen years old, but he was anxious to get away from home as well as be a hero.

"She was a beauty in her day, had every man in the county interested in her. Then she up and married Flap Whittaker, who was just about the puniest man around. Everybody was shocked but, by and by, they come to understand that she wanted a weak man. Partly to boss him and mostly because she was vain—loved to look at herself in the mirror. I suppose with a wallflower of a husband, she could still be the plumb center of attention.

"Well, her son set off to make his way in the world. Despite his young age, he was a good shot and convinced the recruiters that he was old enough to fight in a war. You can imagine his mother was just sick with worry, him not only running off on her, but actually going into battle. He wrote pretty regular, and by some miracle got through four years of that bloody war without being shot up. Meantime his mother went pretty near crazy worrying about him.

"But once the war ended, he wrote to her that he was coming home directly. She was happy for the first time in them whole four years. She told her little hen-pecked husband to spruce up their place, and she planned a big homecoming picnic.

"Well, they waited one week. And then another. Finally a soldier come riding a black horse through the gate to their farm. The old lady rushed out of the house, thinking it was her Cyrus, but she stopped cold when she didn't recognize him. As it turned out, the soldier had been sent to tell her that her son had been killed two days after the war had ended. As he'd been walking home happy as a lark, a Confederate sniper hiding up in a tree had shot the boy dead. The sniper had been living in the wilds so long that he didn't know the war was over.

"Well, the old lady went mad with grief. She kept on wailing, 'Come home, Cyrus. Hurry on home.' She was so out of her mind that she didn't hardly even acknowledge it when her boy was brought home in a wooden coffin and buried up there in the Spring Hill Cemetery with all the other Civil War veterans from Varnell County."

As usual, when Mr. Satterly had finished his story, the young folks, including Hank and Clifford, stood there in a state of awe and wonder. And as usual, Clifford was the first

75

to speak. He stuck his chest out and declared, "That's a right good story, but I don't know whether to believe the half of it or not."

Mr. Satterly squinted at him. "Likely you'll believe me if you go on up to the Historical Society. They got all the boy's letters on file there, and sweet ones they was. They also got some newspaper articles telling how he died, and how his mother went mad, and died herself not six months later. The only thing they never figured out is what happened to the old lady's body."

"Her body?" asked Clifford, his mouth dropping open.

"Yessir. When Mrs. Whittaker died, her sister come in and they laid out her body on the dining room table, with quarters on the eyelids to keep them shut. That was how they done it in them days—had the wake in the house. The old lady was to be buried up the hill in the family graveyard, but during the night, a howling commenced. Wind blasted through the house, knocking over vases and furniture, busting everything, all except the old lady's favorite mirror. Everybody run for their lives, and no one dared to return that night.

"In the morning, a few brave souls crept forward, and they found that the old lady's body had vanished. Ever since then her ghost has appeared in the window, and she calls out to her son."

Hank grinned uneasily. "Well, I wouldn't ever go up there at night, that's for sure. But it can't be too dangerous during the day, can it, 'long as I keep my distance from that old spook house?"

"You still be careful," Mr. Satterly said. "There's nothing on this earth more powerful than a mother's love for her child. I don't know what I could do to save you, if that old lady was to catch hold of you."

Hank heeded Mr. Satterly's advice, keeping to the tractor lane as he walked toward the old Whittaker house. In the distance he could see its dull gray clapboards in the gloomy April afternoon, the black rectangles of its windows drinking up the light. As he passed, he quickened his step, and was just about to put the house behind him when a bolt of lightning flashed directly above it in the blackening sky.

Hank stood in shock, gazing at the house, then started to run away, just as an intensely dark storm front rolled in, smothering the light and discharging flash after flash of lightning. On the ground, a strange white fog gathered around him, drifting in so thick that he couldn't see the tractor lane.

At the risk of running into the barbed wire fence or tripping into the ditch, he hightailed it away from the house, but still he heard the voice of the old lady, laughing and crying at the same time, it seemed to him. "I've got to get out of here," he whispered desperately to himself. But no matter how hard he ran the voice seemed to gain on him, until its moaning was next to his ear. "Cy-rus. Come home, son. Cy-rus!"

"I'm not Cyrus!" he shouted back, short of breath.

"Yes, you are."

"I am not!"

"Why, you're the very image of him. Come here, son. Look into my mirror."

"No! I'm not going anywhere near you. Just leave me alone!"

Hank was certain that he must be near home now, when suddenly a crack of lightning overhead lit up the gray Whittaker house—directly in front of him. The thunder that followed was so loud it seemed the very sky was breaking apart.

The ghost lady stood on the porch in a long tattered dress. Shrunken, her face caved in, she had only black holes where her eyes had once been. She said formally, "Come in, my son. Rest your legs. You must be exhausted from all your travels to distant places."

"No!" Hank screamed. "Let me go! I want to go home!"

"I've been waiting such a long time for you, Cyrus. Over a hundred years."

The faster Hank worked his legs in an effort to retreat, the more quickly he was propelled toward the ghost lady. "Every night I've burned a candle in the window for you," she said. "I've kept your room for you, Cyrus, exactly as it always was."

"I'm not Cyrus!"

Ignoring his protests, she flung her shriveled arms around him, entangling him in the strands of her white hair, like spider webs. Turning her brownish- purple lips to him, she said, "Give your dear mother a kiss."

"No!"

He struggled furiously to escape the grasp of her cold, leathery arms, and especially to avoid those withered lips.

She cackled, "What, no kiss for your dear old mother? I know you've been off soldiering. Now I suppose you think you're too much of a grown man to give your mother one little kiss."

"Let me go!"

The ghost lady snapped, "Not on your life, you ungrateful child!"

Abruptly, she whisked Hank inside the house, and up the stairs to a dust-whitened bedroom. He found himself locked in the room, sitting on the bed, amid walls papered in a flower pattern of mournful blue. There was a wash basin and old furniture, including a brass bed like one he'd once seen in a museum in Indianapolis. He tried to open the door, but when he turned the knob he found that he had no strength. He next tried to shatter the glass of the window, but was able to do little more than touch the pane. He felt as if he were trapped in a dream, in which terrible things happened to him and he was absolutely powerless to prevent them. He called out, but he had no voice.

"You're mine now!" the ghost lady shrieked. "All mine again!"

Inside the room was utterly quiet, although outside the lightning shattered the dark, and the wind became so violent that it snatched his breath away. Meanwhile, all around him, the ghost lady howled in triumph.

He moved about the room, unable to touch anything, as if he had become a ghost himself.

"You're back with me now," the ghost lady said, as if she could read his thoughts. "Don't you see, you're safe now, Cyrus. All you have to do is look into my mirror."

"I'm not Cyrus," Hank tried to tell her again, as she thrust the mirror in front of his face. He couldn't utter a sound, and he was barely able to avert his gaze just in time from the mirror.

"Stubborn boy!" she cried, drifting through the door. "You should know that you have no power over me."

Gradually the room darkened, and Hank was left with the creaking night sounds of the old house, and a wailing far off into the distance, as if someone were in extraordinary pain. Huddled on the bed, in the dark, he was held in utter terror. Later that night, he thought he heard the voices of two people quarreling in the other room. He crept to the door, peeked through the keyhole, and saw the lady and the ghost of an old man in old-timey clothes encrusted with clods of dirt.

The old man begged, "Come along, Flossie."

"I can't!" cried the ghost lady. "Our Cyrus is home now. He needs me to take care of him."

"That's not our Cyrus," the old man said. "Come now, Flossie. Let yourself be buried up at the family graveyard, right along side of me, which is where you rightfully belong."

"Not without my boy!"

The old man flared. "I tell you that's not our Cyrus! You can't take him with you, and if you leave him in there he'll just die like all the others."

The ghost lady wrung her hands. "Don't you see, I can't rest. Not until my Cyrus is back with me." And she set to howling "Cy-rus!" so eerily that Hank was driven back to the bed. They've all perished in here, he thought, and unless I find a way out, I'll die here too. He sat there in shock, until he heard a light tapping on the door, and the ghost lady entered with a tray. "I thought you'd like a little refreshment," she said cheerfully.

Hank surveyed the corn muffins with raspberry preserves, and the small pitcher of buttermilk. He hadn't eaten in many hours and by rights he should have been famished, but he had no appetite, just a sick feeling in the depths of his stomach. "I'm not hungry," he told the ghost lady. "Just leave me alone."

"But you've got to eat. You've got to keep up your strength for our journey."

"What journey?"

Her mouth twisted into the semblance of a smile. "I'm taking you with me, my dear."

81

"Where?"

"To the grave, of course, Cyrus."

"I'm not going anywhere with you!"

"If you don't, you'll die just the same, like the rest of them. Do it for your dear old mother's sake. Come look into my mirror. Please?"

Hank was about to offer another protest when he noticed that she had left the door ajar. Quick as light, he ran for it, the ghost lady shrieking, "You come back here!" He bounded down the stairs, but immediately found himself in a labyrinth of halls. Like an icy wind, the ghost lady rushed after him. The furniture slid back and forth around the room and the family pictures rattled on the wall, as if all of the ghost lady's ancestors were being called to join in the hunt.

Directly behind him, with twisted, yellow fingernails raised, the ghost lady clawed at Hank, repeatedly shrieking, "Come back here!" Hank tried one door after another, but they were either locked or led nowhere. "Cyrus, don't act this way!" Lunging at him, she caught him with those long nails, just as he rammed his shoulder against a door which unexpectedly burst open. Headlong, he tumbled down a flight of stairs into a gloomy basement.

The walls and ceiling were white with cobwebs which caught at Hank's hair and face. As he wiped them away, his eyes grew more accustomed to the dark, and he noticed skeletons strewn throughout the room. "See!" the ghost lady shouted triumphantly down the stairs. "See what's going to happen to you for scorning me, your own mother! They were all boys like you. Now come back up here! There's no way to escape me!"

The last thing on earth Hank wanted to do was what the ghost lady bade him, but deciding that he had no choice, he climbed back up the stairs and returned to the room she had prepared for him. The ghost lady howled throughout the house, as though she inhabited every nook and cranny.

Hank tumbled into a profound sleep, and when he awoke in the depths of night, he was certain that it had been a dream. But then he realized he was locked in the room. Presently the ghost lady materialized in the doorway. "Sleep well?" she asked.

Hank glanced away from her.

"Are you ready to go with me now?"

"No."

"You just have to look into my mirror. We'll be carried away to the grave, and finally we'll both be safe and sound."

"I'm not going with you," Hank contended. "Leave me alone."

The ghost lady flew at Hank in a rage. "How dare you speak to me in that tone! I see you need a lesson in good manners, like all the other boys. Either come with me, or go into the cellar with them!" She pursued him around the room, Hank barely able to elude the grasp of her yellowed fingernails. He was near exhaustion when he heard a car door slam out in the yard.

The ghost lady stopped abruptly. "What was that?" she demanded, then rushed out of the room, locking the door behind her.

Through the window, Hank glimpsed Mr. Satterly, Sheriff Rollins, and Clifford getting out of the patrol car. They stood in the yard in front of the house, Clifford positioning himself well behind the two men.

Frantically, Hank waved to get their attention, but they didn't seem to be able to see him. He must be invisible, he concluded.

"I'm here! I'm here!" he cried futilely, but it appeared that they couldn't hear him either.

Sheriff Rollins grumbled to Mr. Satterly, "I don't know why this couldn't have waited 'til morning."

Mr. Satterly stared at the house and said, "I know the boy is trapped in there somewheres. It's not like him to stay out all night."

Sheriff Rollins grumbled, "If this is some kind of wild goose chase . . ."

Clifford just stood there shaking from head to foot, like a small dog with fleas.

Hank's hopes rose as they clumped into the house and wandered from room to room, but they never found him. It was as if the room in which he was imprisoned didn't exist in the material world. He seemed to be in some strange dimension between the real and the supernatural. Finally they walked back outside where the sheriff complained, "This place gives me the willies. Let's get the heckfire out of here."

"Good idea," said Clifford.

Mr. Satterly frowned at him. "I thought Hank was your friend."

"Well, he was," Clifford said. "But as long as he's dead, which I expect he is, we ought to just hightail it out of here."

Old Mr. Satterly mumbled an apology in the general direction of the house, "I'm sorry, Hank. I should've never let you pass by this old spook house, even in the daylight. I know you're in there somewheres. I can just feel it in my bones. But I don't know how to get you free."

Meanwhile, Clifford had jumped in the car and was urging the old man, "Hurry up before it gets us too!"

Hank's hopes plummeted as he watched Sheriff Rollins and Mr. Satterly climb into the car as well.

"You're mine now!" the ghost lady cackled. "And you're going to suffer, boy, just as you've made me suffer these long years. Now you'll know pain. Real pain."

Hank struggled to free himself, but she possessed the uncanny power of spirits.

Then through the window, he heard Mr. Satterly call, "Old woman, I know you're in there!"

"What's that?" the ghost lady demanded. "I thought the fools had left." She rushed to the window and there were the sheriff and Mr. Satterly again.

Waiting in the car, Clifford said to the two men. "We already searched once. Let's get the heck out of here!"

Holding up an old newspaper clipping, Mr. Satterly declared, "I know you got Hank in there, old lady. But he ain't your boy!"

"Then where is my boy?" the ghost lady shrieked, rattling the glass in the windows.

Sheriff Rollins' eyes bugged out, and Clifford dove under the dashboard.

Swallowing hard, Mr. Satterly shouted, "He's buried up in the Spring Hill Cemetery along with all the other Civil War veterans. And I got proof. It says so right here in this newspaper article."

"But he belongs up here with me. He ought to be buried beside me in the family plot."

"Well, I can't do nothing about that!"

"You can have him moved."

"Will you set Hank free if I do?"

"Never!"

The word rang in Hank's ears. He just stood there in shock.

"Why not?" asked Mr. Satterly.

"He's a no-account good-for-nothing, just like those other boys in the cellar. My Cyrus was a good boy."

Scratching the stubble on his chin, Mr. Satterly appeared to be pondering some deep question. Then he marched resolutely into the house.

"Where are you going?" shrieked the ghost lady. "This is my house and you were not invited in." When Mr. Satterly didn't answer, she flew down the stairs to confront him.

Trailing after her, looking for a chance to run for his life, Hank found Mr. Satterly in the parlor, holding the oval mirror high over his head.

The ghost lady gasped, "What do you think you're doing?"

"I'm going to shatter this mirror."

"You'll bring a nightmare upon yourself if you so much as scratch that mirror!" the ghost lady warned. "You'll release spirits far worse than me!"

"I'm going to shatter it, vain woman," said Mr. Satterly, cocking an eye at her. "But first I want you to take a good look at yourself!" He thrust the mirror directly in front of Flossie Whittaker.

"Who is that hideous creature?" she cried. "Get her away from me!"

"That's you!" Mr. Satterly answered.

"It can't be. I'm young and beautiful."

"Not anymore. Now be gone with you!" Mr. Satterly said, shattering the oval mirror on the floor.

"No! No! No!" screamed the ghost lady as the house shuddered and cracks split along the plaster walls.

"Hurry, son!" Mr. Satterly called to Hank as the ancient walls began to crumble around them.

They slipped out of the house just as it violently erupt-
ed and then collapsed upon itself. "Now get into your grave,
vain woman!" Mr. Satterly shouted into the wreckage. "And
don't bother the living ever again!"

Suddenly the night went calm. Stars littered the sky and
Hank found that he could speak again. "What happened,
Mr. Satterly?" he asked.

"She's gone, I think."

"Are you sure?" squeaked Clifford, who crept out of the
patrol car.

"Well, there's only one way to be sure," said Mr. Satterly. "We got to go out back to the family graveyard. Come on,
Clifford."

"Me? Maybe I ought to stay here and watch the car."

"Good idea," Mr. Satterly said. "In case the ghost lady's
still around."

"Then again, you might need me," Clifford said.

"Although maybe we ought to come back in the morning," he suggested, glancing over his shoulder. "We'll be
able to see lots better in the daytime."

"Just what are you thinking?" asked Sheriff Rollins, as
the four of them walked across the yard to the small family
graveyard tucked in the far corner of the pasture.

"I want to be sure it's over, once and for all," Mr. Satterly explained.

The last place on earth Hank wanted to visit was that
family graveyard, but he went along with them to the scrap
of meadow, surrounded by a square of iron fence. Several
chalky white stones glowed in the moonlight.

"Look there!" Mr. Satterly gasped, pointing to a grave.
"There she lies!"

The marker over Flossie Whittaker's grave looked to be very weathered, with the dates reading "1829-1865," and an inscription stating, "Here lies a woman who loved more than she could endure." However, the grave itself appeared to have been freshly dug.

"Think she'll stay put?" Hank asked, as they headed back to the car, Clifford well out in front of them.

Mr. Satterly nodded. "I reckon so."

"But how did you know about the mirror? That's what I'd like to know," asked Sheriff Rollins.

Mr. Satterly rubbed his chin. "Well, I didn't rightly know for sure. It was just a hunch. What I figured was that nobody could really love their child in that way, not truly love them. Otherwise she would have let him go. I figured that when it come right down to it, a woman like that must have actually loved herself a sight more than anything else, including her son. And the only thing really keeping her from the grave was her own vanity."

"I don't care who or what was keeping her from her grave," Hank said. "Right now I just want to get out of here!"

Sticking his chest out, Clifford asked, "What's the hurry?"

"Why don't you stay here, Clifford," Mr. Satterly suggested. "You can keep watch on the place to make sure the ghost lady doesn't rise up again."

"Me?" Clifford fumbled. "By myself? Uh, I would, you know I would, except I'm awful tired. It's been a pretty long night for us, rescuing Hank and all."

Sheriff Rollins clapped Clifford on the shoulder. "I guess Mr. Satterly couldn't have done it without you."

Clifford shrugged. "Gosh, it weren't nothing."

You can say that again, thought Hank.

As the four of them climbed into the car and drove away from the Whittaker house, Hank asked Mr. Satterly, "You think we should, you know, have her son dug up and buried next to her?"

Mr. Satterly spat out the car window. "No, sir."

"Why not?"

"I figure the boy went into the army of his own choice. According to his letters, he liked it there, at least being away from home, and being with the friends he chose, and serving honorably with them. So I figure he ought to be buried where he wants to be."

"That makes sense to me," said Hank. "Sort of."

Mr. Satterly's eyes twinkled. "If we rebury the boy next to her, who knows? He might start raising a ruckus himself, and then where would we be? No sir, with a mother like his, I expect a young feller would look forward to a little peace and quiet, especially when it's for eternity."

Old Nobb

"**H**ow come the old Nobb Farm is haunted?"
Clifford asked Mr. Satterly one evening late in
June.

A group of young folks, including Hank Cantrell, Rosie Morgan, and Mary Ethel Freeny, were gathered around the old man on the liars' bench in front of Tremont's Drugstore and Fountain.

The old man sighed. "Well now, Clifford, that's a complicated story, and I'm not sure anyone knows the whole of it. But I was acquainted with Ephraim Nobb. I even met his mother, with whom he lived his whole entire life. In fact, when we was boys, my brothers and I once worked for the man."

Clifford's eyes got as big as baseballs. "Really? On that spooky old farm?"

Mr. Satterly nodded. "For a fact, and it was just as spooky back then. Old Nobb never did believe in paint, and the house and all the outbuildings were weathered gray. He didn't believe in yard work either, and the weeds were waist deep or higher all around the farm, except for little trails he and his hogs had beat down over the years."

"How come you worked for him?" Clifford asked eagerly.

"Well, I'm getting to that now, ain't I? So hold your horses. You see, when my brothers and I were boys, our father not only kept us busy at home, but he also liked to loan us out to neighbors as a sign of his generosity. My older brother Whitcomb, my younger brother Jug, and myself never particularly appreciated the gesture. Partly because our father was so uninterested in work himself that we were already plenty busy doing all the work on our own farm. And partly because, knowing our neighbors, we guessed they would be more than tempted to take advantage of us.

"Ephraim Nobb, who thankfully lived downwind of us, had just enough acreage to raise hogs, and he was so unsuccessful at this venture that he needed extra hands in a bad way. He was a scrawny man, with a perpetual smirk on his face. And he was so stingy that he saved money by cutting his own hair with a pair of bent scissors. And without benefit of a mirror, judging from the jagged line of hair that ran across his forehead, down either side of the head to halfway over his ears, and below the back of his old beat-up fedora hat.

He also got the most out of his razor blades, using them but once or twice a week. A single pair of overalls and workshirt, along with the fedora scrunched down on his head, were all the clothes he had in this world. On washdays, which didn't occur often, we heard that he went around in his long underwear, which he wore year round, no matter how hot the weather.

"He wasn't able to afford actual pens for his hogs, so he'd knocked apart shipping crates that he'd gotten free from the freight yards over in Boggsville, and built his own hodgepodge which he held together with baling wire and hope. These pens held a remarkable assortment of hogs—white hogs, red hogs, black hogs. He had black hogs with white belts and vice versa, not to mention spotted hogs of every imaginable combination of colors.

"Some folks argued that his hogs were bred with wild animals, while others contended that they broke out of their makeshift pens so often that they had just reverted to their wild origins.

"They was certainly lively, especially the boars with their yellow tusks. The crowns of their hairy backs rose practically to a man's chest. They absolutely despised people except as possible food. The boars spent their days busting into each other's pens to snort and gouge at each other, their wounds bright with blood in the afternoon sun.

"Old Nobb's method worked to some extent—his sows produced extraordinarily large litters of multi-colored piglets. However, by the time they were ready for market, half the hogs had run off into the woods. Of course, my dad felt sorry for Old Nobb. He would shake his head, muttering, 'Poor old Nobb. He needs our help, boys.' And he would send Whitcomb, Jug, and me over to the man's farm.

"Mostly my brothers and me hauled his corn, barley, and oats to the elevator so the old codger could have it ground and mixed into his own 'secret feed,' as he called it. Old Nobb never caught on to the value of owning a wagon and horses, especially when his neighbors was so willing to let him use theirs, complete with hired help.

"From time to time we also helped him round up his hogs, which lent an air of excitement to the afternoon. More than once an angry hog turned on me, clamped its jaws on my ankle, and yanked me to the ground. I always scrambled out of the way before I got mauled. But we had drawn worse assignments and were counting our blessings when one August afternoon, Old Nobb suggested that we help him clean hog pens. 'I could sure use your help,' he explained, 'seein's how it's never been done before.'

"'What are neighbors for?' our father said, waving his hand graciously. 'We'll be glad to help, won't we, boys! Boys?'

"Knowing the depth of manure in the pens, we balked at this particular proposal, insisting that we be paid.

"'Paid?' asked Old Nobb, apparently not acquainted with the practice.

"'Yeah,' Whitcomb, my oldest brother, protested. 'That's goin' to be one heck of a job.'

"'And it's gol'derned hot,' said Jug.

"'Not to mention the flies,' I pointed out.

"Old Nobb spat a black comet of tobacco juice into the dust at our feet, muttering, 'Well, all right.'

"We stood there amazed that he'd agreed so readily. Whitcomb explained, 'We usually get a dollar a day—each.'

"His eyes sparkling, his big grin exposing toothless gums, Nobb said, 'Don'choo boys worry yourselves none. I'll do you even better than a dollar a day.'

"All week Whitcomb, Jug, and I shoveled pig manure in sheer ecstasy. Real money was something hard to come by in Varnell County, especially in those days, and we imagined holding it in our very own hands. Of course, it was the hottest week in August, and the time when the flies were the thickest. And the smell! My Lord!

"Old Nobb had borrowed an iron-wheeled tractor from Bud Wolfert and a manure spreader from Leroy Sadler, and the three of us filled it again and again, 'til we lost count. The pig manure stood a good foot deep in each of them pens and threatened to suck us down like quicksand. Needless to say, the hogs didn't appreciate the intrusion either.

"But what the heck, we were about to have us some real cash money!

"On Friday, toward noon, we were finally completing our assignment, hoping that after a proper washing Mom would let us back into the house. We was just rinsing ourselves off as best we could under the hand pump when Old Nobb come ambling through the weeds. He grinned at us. 'You boys done right good work. Today you can have dinner with me and Ma.'

"Even if I had tried—which I had never wanted to—I could never have imagined what his mother might feed us. In the first place, I had never seen the woman, since she remained in the house all the time.

"My brothers and I looked at each other. We were too hot and exhausted to come up with an excuse, so before we knew it, we found ourselves being escorted into that dank gray house with cardboard nailed over the windows.

"Mrs. Nobb seemed likeable enough, although with her pale skin she was as faded as her old, washed-out calico dress. She met us at the door, saying, 'Come in, boys. Make yourselfs at home.'

"To save on heat in the winters, they'd boarded up all the rooms, except for the kitchen and the parlor, which were separated by a blanket hung on a piece of clothesline. Perhaps most remarkable was their tablecloth which was made of stitched-together plastic bread wrappers.

"My brothers and I laughed nervously as we walked into the house and sat down at the table. We were relieved to be served simple pork burgers—or what we hoped was pork. We also had pickled watermelon rind, green beans, and fried potatoes, all of which I prayed wouldn't give us pto-maine poisoning. Although I ate every bite, I was so desperate to get out of there, I didn't taste any of it.

"Not having said more than a couple dozen words to us all summer, Old Nobb fell into a talkative mood as we finished dinner and strolled out onto the porch, which tilted forward at a steep angle toward the front yard. He knocked the ashes from his pipe, refilled the bowl with a substance that looked like compost, and insisted that we set down and rest a spell.

"We did as he requested, staring into the dazzling white of that August afternoon, no one able to think of a thing to say, except Old Nobb who abruptly asked, 'Did you boys know I was married once? Yessir, I was. But she up and left me.' He drew on the pipe and stared off into the middle distance. 'To this day, I ain't figured out why.'

"My brothers and I remained prudently silent.

"'Yep, she moved somewhere up north. Well, that's neither here nor there now,' Old Nobb said, slapping his knee, in the process raising a cloud of gray dust. 'Guess we oughten to settle up now.' At that our spirits rose considerably. By our reckoning we was owed eleven dollars each. However, instead of giving us cash money, he walked us back to the hog lot, reached in, and solemnly presented each of us with a little runt pig with spindly legs and a long thin snout like a tap root.

"'But you said we'd get better than a dollar a day! These pigs ain't worth a dollar each,' Whitcomb argued. 'You owe each of us eleven dollars.'

"Old Nobb winked at us. 'But you take these here pigs and raise 'em up, let 'em have a litter or two, and they'll make you better'n eleven dollars.'

"I suppose there was some consolation in the fact that we refused to ever work for Ephraim Nobb again. Our father reminded us that he was a poor old man and told us that we should be ashamed of our lack of gratitude. I did feel a touch badly, because Old Nobb certainly didn't have much of a life.

"Well, the years went by, and I read in the newspaper that his mother died. And a few years after that, I read that Old Nobb himself had passed away, leaving close to a hundred thousand dollars stuffed away in the walls of his house!"

"A hundred thousand dollars?" asked Clifford in amazement.

"Yessir," said Mr. Satterly. "Can you imagine that? All them years of living dirt poor in that tumbledown house, hoarding his money, with no electricity or indoor plumbing. He and his mother used an outhouse to their dying day."

"What happened to the money?" asked Clifford.

"It went to charity. Which would have infuriated Old Nobb, since he was just about the stingiest man on God's green earth, despite what he asked of others."

"How could he accumulate so much money?" asked Rosie. "Wasn't that an awful lot of money back then?"

"It was then, and it is now," Mr. Satterly said. "But it must have been pretty easy for him since he never spent a nickel. He hardly ever bought tools and equipment, since he could borrow them from his neighbors. And as my brothers and I found out, he never hired help, at least for a wage. It just goes to show you, things ain't always what they appear to be."

"But how come the farm is haunted?" asked Mary Ethel.

Mr. Satterly grinned. "Folks say that he has even more

97

money stashed away in that old house, that they never found it all. His ghost is there to keep people from getting it."

At the conclusion of Mr. Satterly's story, Hank and Clifford drifted off along the square with Rosie and Mary Ethel.

The moment Clifford opened his mouth, Hank warned him, "Don't say it."

"Say what?"

"You know exactly what. You want to visit the Nobb Farm, and see if we can find the rest of Ephraim Nobb's money."

"I do not."

"You don't?"

"'Course not. I was just going to ask if you guys wanted to go over to the cafe for a cherry Coke."

Hank couldn't believe it, but the four of them went ahead to the cafe and ordered cherry Cokes. As usual, Clifford didn't have any money, and Hank had to pay for all of them.

They slid into the booth next to the window and as he put a straw into his Coke, Clifford said, "'Course we could just kind of drive by the old Nobb Farm this evening, just for a look-see."

Hank snorted, "I knew it!"

"Knew what?"

"That once you'd heard about Ephraim Nobb's money, you wouldn't be able to get it out of your head."

"We could at least look for it," Clifford suggested. "What are you afraid of?"

Hank reared back. "What am I afraid of? What about you always running off?"

"What do you mean? I've stood my ground every time," Clifford lied, enormously.

"Now that's a lie and a half," Hank said. It was obvious to him that his friend was a coward of the highest order, but the girls didn't seem too certain.

"And I can prove I ain't scared," Clifford went on. "You're the one who never wants to do anything that's the least little bit dangerous. Whereas I'm always game." He turned to the girls. "Am I right, or am I right?"

Mary Ethel squirmed and gazed adoringly at him. "'Course you are, Cliffie."

Rosie added, "He's got a point, Hank. At least he always does want to go to all of these haunted places."

Hank scowled. "But he always runs off at the first whisper of danger."

Clifford shrugged. "I'm just too wily to get caught. Can I help it if you keep getting yourself trapped?"

Hank was sick of Clifford's bragging, but this time he had an idea. "I'll go. We'll all go," he said. "That way you girls can see for yourselves how brave ol' Cliffie is. We'll just stand back and watch him explore the Nobb Farm."

Clifford had gone white as skim milk. "You mean tonight?"

"Right this minute!" Hank declared, slapping the table with the palm of his hand. "Come on, time's a-wasting."

The girls agreed that the proposed visit would constitute a fair test, but Clifford gulped. "Gosh, I'd sure like to, except I almost forgot. There's this show I want to watch on TV tonight."

"What is it?" asked Hank.

"Uh, I forget, but I remember that I wanted to see it real bad."

"Come on," urged Mary Ethel. "We'll show 'em how brave you are, Cliffie."

They badgered Clifford into the pickup and, with the four of them sandwiched into the cab, drove out into the dark countryside.

There was something about the hills, Hank thought as they rode along, that swallowed up the light. You got this feeling that if you strayed from the headlights, you would fall into the bottomless black space pressing all around you.

Old Nobb had only thirty acres at the height of his farming career, and it was amazing that he had amassed such a fortune on such a pathetic scrap of land. Leached by rains, the soil was a very pale gray color, with jagged gullies cutting through the slopes, out of which sprang milkweed and blue thistle. The ground was so poor that no one had bothered to take up residence there in the fifty years since his death, and the tumbledown house, corncrib, hog shed, and barn were now deeply sunk in the tall raggedy undergrowth.

Hank eased the pickup onto the road shoulder, and the four of them followed a dry gully, ducking under branches, until they came to the porch, which tilted forward in the general direction of the front yard. The wind swished through the leaves that fluttered about their faces, while the old abandoned house groaned and creaked as if it were in deep pain.

Clutching his arm, Rosie confessed, "I'm scared, Hank."

Although Hank was tingling himself, he snorted, "Don't worry. Old Cliffie's here. He'll protect us."

Clifford, though, was hanging onto Mary Ethel for dear life. Hank told him, "You go first."

"Me?"

"You want to show everyone how brave you are, don't you? If you look hard enough, you might find that treasure. That way you'll be able to spring for the Cokes next time."

Clifford gulped. "How 'bout you? You want to show everyone how brave you are too, don't you, Hank?"

"That's right," added Mary Ethel. "For all we know, you're scared, too."

"Yeah," Clifford urged. "You go first, unless you're chicken."

Hank sighed. From past experience, he knew that Clifford would stall until next morning, so he grumbled, "All right, I'll go first, but Clifford better come in right after me."

"Of course I will," Clifford said. "What kind of friend do you think I am anyway? I'll be right behind you. Except wait—maybe I ought to stay here to protect Mary Ethel and Rosie."

Hank snorted as he stepped onto the porch, the floorboards groaning beneath his feet. He crept forward to the door which he pushed open, its hinges screeching in torment.

"Be careful," Rosie urged.

The moment Hank stepped inside, the door snapped powerfully shut, and the entire house shuddered with the blow. In terror, he grabbed the white porcelain doorknob, but the screws were loose and it twisted off. "Open the door, Clifford!" he called. "I don't want to get trapped in here."

Out on the porch, Clifford stood, as if in a trance.

"Help him, Clifford," Mary Ethel urged.

"Come on! Don't be a coward," Rosie told him.

Clifford didn't budge.

"Okay, I'll do it myself," Rosie said.

Through the door, Hank could hear her step forward

and try the knob on her side. "It's stuck, Hank," she called through the gray panels of the door.

"Look for something to pry it open with! And hurry!" Hank begged, just as the stale air began to swirl around him, arousing the dust of ages. "Let me out," a high feminine voice whispered softly from the back of the house. "Please let me out."

Mesmerized by the anguished tone of the voice, Hank asked, "Where are you? Who are you?"

A door at the back of the front room creaked open, and he crept toward a dim light, hoping for a way out. He thought he saw the flash of a shadow disappearing into the other room. Around him, the flowered wallpaper hung in tatters. In places, the plaster was stripped away, exposing the wooden lath. Hank's footsteps echoed hollowly in the empty rooms. His very breath seemed to resound off the walls again and again, coming back to him many times amplified.

"Let me out," the voice called from the back room. "Oh, please let me out."

Cautiously, Hank crept forward. Through the doorway he spied an ancient man with roughly-cut hair and toothless gums, rocking in a corner. "Let me out!" the voice called again from somewhere above them.

"Never mind her," the old man said. At Hank's approach his eyes sparkled. "That's just Mama, and she don't know what she's saying. You c'mere, boy. You're just what I been looking for—somebody to help me out in the hog yard."

The man, who was apparently the ghost of Ephraim Nobb, glowed like phosphorous. Breathlessly Hank told him, "There aren't any hogs out there."

"Well, there sure used to be!" the ghost of Old Nobb snapped. "And how the folks used to make fun of me. But I showed 'em. I saved a fortune, and all of it sweated out of fools—fools just like you!" He cackled, then went dead serious as he squinted hard at Hank. "But then what did they do? Once I'd died, they up and throw'd it away on charity!"

Hank asked, "What's so bad about that? After all, you got the money through the charity of your neighbors."

"It was mine!" Old Nobb shouted. "Every red cent! It was downright insulting. It would have been a sight better if they'd have burnt the money."

"I've heard of miserly people before. . . ." Hank said.

"Am I?" Old Nobb asked indignantly. "And you probably come after the rest of my money, but you'll never live long enough to find it!" Snatching up a pitchfork from beside his rocker, Old Nobb jabbed at Hank.

The young man stumbled back into the front room and desperately tried the door again. Pounding on the door, he shouted, "Clifford? Rosie? Help me!"

"Help him, Clifford!" Rosie cried. "He's in danger!"

Clifford whimpered, "He's just clowning around. You know, trying to scare us."

"Old Nobb's after me!" Hank yelled.

"We've got to get this door open," Rosie cried.

"Yeah, come on, Cliffie," urged Mary Ethel. "Show everybody how brave you are."

Coming up behind him, Old Nobb thrust the pitchfork at Hank, who was forced to flee up the stairs. As he retreated, he heard Clifford explaining to the girls, "We don't want to get caught in there, too. We ought to just go for help. Yeah, that's what we ought do."

Rosie tried the knob again. Amazingly, the door opened easily, and the two girls crept into the house, leaving Clifford on the porch.

"Hank?" Rosie called in the gloom.

Meanwhile, Hank had raced through the upstairs hallway and down the backstairs which led into the kitchen. Seeing Rosie and Mary Ethel in the other room, he rushed toward them. "Run for your lives! Old Nobb's after me. He's got a pitchfork!" Suddenly some floorboards caved in, and Hank sank down to his knees.

"Hank?" Rosie cried. Rushing into the kitchen, she dipped beside him. "Are you all right?"

He winced with pain. "Yeah, except my leg is jammed between these boards."

"Don't worry, we'll get you out," Rosie assured him.

Hank shook his head. "Old Nobb's around here. Maybe you'd better escape while you've got a chance."

"If we just had a board or pipe or something to pry these floorboards loose," Rosie said desperately. "Let me look on the back porch."

"Hurry!" Hank urged. "And be careful you don't fall through the floor, too. It's rotting away in a lot of places." Even as Hank spoke, a white shadow flashed past him.

Where had Old Nobb gone, he wondered?

Rosie and Mary Ethel slipped out onto the back porch, where they found an old milkcan, some Ball Mason canning jars, and ancient firewood from another generation. "Here's an old ax," Rosie said. "Maybe we can use the handle to pry loose one of those boards."

Returning with the ax, the girls wedged it into the boards and tried to pry them apart. As hard as the girls pushed, they couldn't move it.

104

"Clifford?" Mary Ethel called. "We need you. Hurry, we need your help."

No answer.

"I can see you clear as day through the doorway," Rosie observed. "Don't just stand there."

Clifford appeared rooted to the porch.

"Come on," Mary Ethel said urgently. "And hurry!"

Again the shadow fluttered over them, as if it were a large moth looking for a place to settle.

Slowly, Clifford backed away.

"Where are you going?" Mary Ethel demanded. "And if you say you're going for help, you better get some for yourself!"

Just then Hank noticed the twisted face of Ephraim Nobb in the yard, peering out from the scrub trees, pitchfork in hand. "Watch out!" he called to his friend.

Old Nobb sprang in front of Clifford, thrust the pitchfork in his face, and demanded, "Where do you think you're going, boy?"

Clifford appeared to be struck dumb.

"Don't think you can get away from me, boy. I need someone to help me around the place."

"But I got to go home," Clifford said, his voice rising to a sharp whine.

"That's what they all say. But you ain't never goin' home, boy. I'm gonna fix it so's you stay here with me and Mama for all eternity. It'll take you that long to pay back the money you was fixin' to steal from me."

"I didn't take any of your money!"

Old Nobb spat vigorously at Clifford's feet. "But you would have, if you only knew where the rest of the money was hid." The old man's face twisted. "Now get over to that barn, and get yourself to work."

"Help!" Clifford cried. "Help me!"

"Shut up!" Old Nobb said, jabbing at him with the pitchfork. "Or I'll poke you so full of holes you'll think you was a sieve."

Inside, in the Nobb kitchen, Rosie and Mary Ethel gave one last tug on the ax handle, and the board splintered around Hank's leg. Pulling free, he briefly inspected the ankle, which was swelling to the size of a hedgeapple. "Let's go," he suggested to the girls as he worked himself to his feet and hobbled to the door.

"What about Cliffie?" asked Mary Ethel, wringing her hands, as they stepped onto the front porch.

"What about him?" said Rosie.

"We've got to try to save him!"

"Like he tried to save Hank?" asked Rosie.

"He's still my little Cliffie."

Hank didn't know what they could do. With his sprained ankle, he could barely stand up, let alone walk. But gripping the ax in his sweaty hands, he limped toward the front doorway.

Again the white shadow fluttered over him, and this time the ghost of an old woman materialized directly in front of him, blocking the doorway. She wore a flowing white nightgown, and her skin was blanched as if she never got any sun.

"Where do you think you're going?" she demanded.

Raising the ax, Hank answered, "Get out of my way."

"But my Ephraim needs you. You see all the work that needs to be done around here."

Hank told her, "It's too late now. He should have done it himself, during all those years when he was alive."

"The girls can help me scrub up the house," she said.

"Out of our way!" Hank ordered, brandishing the ax.

"You think that ax will do you any good?" the old lady chortled, sweeping her hand through the blade as if it weren't there.

Hank lowered the ax, but he kept thinking that there must be a way to defeat the ghost of Mrs. Nobb. "All right," he sighed at length. "Show the girls where the mops and buckets are, and I'll go help your son in the barn."

The old lady smiled, her teeth as yellowed as her long waxen fingernails. "Very well."

The moment she stepped out of the doorway, Hank grabbed Rosie and Mary Ethel by the arms and hollered, "Run for your lives!" They fled through the brush, he limping after them.

"Come back here!" shrieked the ghost of Mrs. Nobb. "You have to stay here and work for us!" Yet she pursued them only as far as the front porch. Pausing in the yard, Hank dared to glance back. "I don't think she can come after us," he said to the girls. "She can't leave the house."

They watched as the ghost of the old lady fluttered like a large moth on the porch, then flew inside, moving from window to window through the house. "Let me out!" she screamed. "Please let me out of here!"

Hobbling through the scrub oaks, Hank said, "You girls go back to the truck, pull it out onto the road, and wait for me."

"What about Cliffie?"

Hank frowned. "I'm going to try to save that dope, although I don't know why." As the girls vanished in the deep foliage, he limped toward the barn, calling, "Ephraim Nobb. Hey, Nobb!"

Hobbling into the wide doorway of the barn, Hank observed the peevish old ghost about to attach a chain to Clifford's leg. Old Nobb glanced up to ask, "What is it? Don't tell me you've come to help me. I seen how you tricked Mama. I've got this boy now, and there ain't nothin' you can do to save him. He's a little on the puny side, but he'll have to do, 'long as I keep him chained up here in the barn."

Hank was already shaking his head. "No sir, I'm not going to help you." Old Nobb's primary weakness, Hank reasoned, was that he was concerned only with his own interests, his own property. So he said, "I just come to tell you that your hogs have got out again."

"My hogs?"

"Yessir. You better get them before they disappear into the woods, or before somebody else comes and claims them for their own."

"They better think twice before they try to take my hogs!" roared Old Nobb. As he stepped out of the barn, Clifford made a break for it.

"Why you!" the ghost of Ephraim Nobb shrieked.

He swooped after the boys, jabbing at them with the pitchfork as they broke for the truck, stumbling down the hill through the scrub oaks and brush. "We're never going to make it!" Clifford whined. "We should never have come here!"

"Shut up and run!" Hank ordered, hopping and wincing with pain from his twisted ankle.

They came to an old barbed wire fence, its rusted strands looped from one hedge post to another. Hobbling on his bad leg, Hank lunged over the fence, Clifford right behind him.

Stopping at the fence, Old Nobb ranted at them. Just to be on the safe side, Hank and Clifford scrambled into the back of the waiting pickup. Rosie hit the gas and, scattering gravel, they tore down the road.

Nobody had much to say that night, especially Clifford, although Hank knew that before long he would bring up the question of the money still hidden on Old Nobb's farm and would want to return there. More precisely, he would want Hank to go back for it.

As for himself, Hank would just as soon remain poor, and alive. He contented himself with thinking about Old Nobb, who had always tricked others into helping him, and of the night he had tricked the ghost of the old farmer in order to help a friend.

Ghost of the Hotel Montezuma

"Come on, you guys," Clifford urged one evening in late April. "I want to show you my new john-boat. She's a beauty. Cost me twenty dollars, but she was worth it, and then some."

Having little else to do, Rosie, Mary Ethel, and Hank agreed to go. They drove over to Boggsville and wandered down to the landing on the Wabash River, where they had a look at the fishing boat that Clifford had been bragging about all evening.

"That's it?" Mary Ethel asked in disgust as, with a flourish of his arm, Clifford indicated his pride and joy. It was nothing more than a stubby rowboat, with peeling blue paint and warped gunnels. "Does it float?" Hank asked.

Clifford reared up. "Of course it does! What do you think it's doing right now? It's the perfect fishing boat. 'Course, I plan to spruce it up a little. Shoot, it doesn't need nothin' more than a little paint."

Cocking his head to the left, Hank squinted at the boat and observed, "Looks a little lopsided, too."

"No, it isn't!" Clifford insisted. "That's just the angle you're looking at it from."

Hank shook his head. "No, it's definitely warped."

"What say we get a Coke," Rosie suggested. "I can't believe we drove all the way over here just to look at that."

"Wait a minute," Clifford protested. "Don't you guys want to take a ride in it?"

"What for?" Hank asked.

"Come on!" Clifford begged. "It's a pretty night. We can just go across the river and back. Then you'll see what a nice boat I got."

Hank studied the sky. "It doesn't look much like rain, but the river's still awful high." They had enjoyed an abundance of rain that spring which had caused the Wabash to spread broadly over the flood plain.

"What're you so worried about?" Clifford asked. "I got a motor for the boat. It's not like we're gonna be swept downstream or nothin'."

Hank was shaking his head as he kicked at a loose board on the dock with the toe of his boot. "I don't know. It's pretty dangerous out there on the river this time of year." There was a quiet power to the Wabash, just beneath its deceptively calm surface—especially during the high-water stage in the spring, when it often overflowed its banks and spread over the surrounding bottom ground and low-lying fields.

However, clasping his arm, Rosie said, "It *is* a pretty night, Hank. What would it hurt if we went for a little boat ride? Mary Ethel and I would like that, wouldn't we, Mary Ethel?"

"Yes, we would indeed," declared Mary Ethel, making eyes at Clifford.

"And I'm an expert boatsman," Clifford added, sticking out his chest as best he could.

"Sure you are," Hank grumbled. "And quit that. You're showing your ribs again."

Clifford went into the boathouse and returned with his motor, which resembled a glorified egg-beater. With an air of importance he hitched it to the rear of the boat, wound a piece of rope around it, and pulled. At first the motor wouldn't start, but on the twentieth yank or so, it sputtered uncertainly, then settled into a low buzz.

"Finally," Rosie sighed.

"That motor looks to be about as powerful as a dragon-fly," Hank observed.

"It even sounds like an insect," Rosie added.

"Grump, grump," Clifford said. "Why can't you guys ever look at things on the positive side?"

"Because we know you too well," Hank said.

They all joined Clifford in the boat, which groaned with their weight, and Hank unhitched it from the dock. Although the boat leaned to the right, Clifford nosed it out into the river as if he were the captain of a cruise ship.

"I hope you got enough gas in that engine," Hank mentioned.

"Gas?" Clifford echoed vaguely.

"Yes," Hank said. "We can't afford to run out of gas, not in these high flood waters. You didn't bring a gas can, so I expect you've got a full tank."

"Uh, sure. Heck, yeah," Clifford said. "You don't think I'd be fool enough to leave without checking the gas." No sooner were the words out of his mouth than the boat was spun in a circle.

As Clifford struggled to maintain control of the boat which was bobbing and rocking vigorously, Hank suggested, "You're getting caught up in the current. Try to steer closer to the bank where the water's a little calmer."

Suddenly the boat whirled to their left, barely avoiding the twisted branch of an oak tree that was being swept downstream. Everyone clung to the gunnels for dear life. As a muddy wave swept over the bow, Clifford blubbered, "We're gonna drown! I just know it! I knew we shouldn't have come out here."

"Then why did you insist on taking this dang boat out?" Hank started to ask, but he knew from experience that Clifford's middle name was "illogical." Instead he cried, "Just point the boat back to the shore, and whatever you do, don't lose your head."

However, they were all terrified as they were swept relentlessly downstream. Then the motor sputtered and died.

"What's the matter?" Hank called to Clifford.

Removing the gas cap and squinting into the hole, Clifford announced, "Uh, I think we're out of gas."

Hank ground his teeth. "I knew it. Quick! Grab the oars!"

"I only got one!" Clifford whined.

"Then give it to me!" Hank ordered.

With the single oar, Hank managed to paddle the boat closer to shore. Gradually, as the flooded river widened, covering vast stretches of low ground, the current relaxed and Hank was able to steer the boat out of the main channel altogether.

They slipped under the Perrysville bridge and before them, the water spread into a moon-whitened lake. "Where are we?" Rosie asked.

"Just above Montezuma, I expect," Hank said, "but I'm not sure. Nothin' around here looks familiar."

"Of course, you can't recognize anything!" Clifford

snapped like a little dog. "With all the floodwater, everything looks different."

"Expert boatsman," Hank grumbled under his breath as he paddled them closer to shore. "We could have all drowned out there."

"Oh, cut it out!" Clifford cried. "Can I help it if the boat just kind of got away from me?"

"You also forgot to check the gas," Mary Ethel reminded him.

"Okay, rub it in," Clifford said. "Some friends you guys are. At least the boat didn't spring a leak."

"Don't even say it," Hank said.

"Well, it didn't," Clifford bragged. "It's as seaworthy as a battleship."

Ignoring him, Mary Ethel observed, "It sure does look different around here."

"But it's so pretty," Rosie noted.

The soft waves wrinkled the reflection of the moon. A ragged line of trees silhouetted the distant shoreline, and the sky had deepened to a purplish-blue color.

"It's almost like we're the only people for miles around," Clifford whispered nervously.

Gradually, the boat settled in the floodwater, far from any bank. "Now what are we going to do?" Rosie asked. "We could be stranded out here all night."

Hank said, "I'll have to paddle us in with this single oar."

"You will?" Clifford asked.

"Of course," Hank said. "If I don't, you'll just sit here whining and complaining all night."

"Well, what else am I supposed to do?" Clifford asked.

"Are you sure you can paddle us all the way to the bank?" Rosie asked Hank.

116

"The bank!" Mary Ethel gasped.

Suddenly, they were no longer in sight of solid ground.

"It can't be," Rosie said, awed. "Even when it's spread across the flood plain, the Wabash isn't so wide that you can't see the bank, at least one of them."

"It's like we've drifted into another world," Clifford remarked, wide-eyed.

The black water appeared to hold their boat still, as a low white fog, suspended just inches above the surface, began to drift around them. Then, just in front of them, the water began to churn violently.

Suddenly, a long wail shattered the night air, and out of the frothy brown water arose the shuddering gray hulk of an old building—first the roof, then the walls shrugging off the silt. It looked like an old clapboard house of Victorian design, except that above its screened-in porch was a sign which read: *Hotel Montezuma.*

"It can't be," Hank gasped as he and Rosie clung to each other.

"What's happening? What is this place?" Rosie asked, her voice breaking.

Hank remembered he had once seen an old sepia-tinted photograph of the hotel, and he had read about it in old newspapers at the Varnell County historical museum. Although shocked by its startling appearance, floating in the water, he managed to tell the others, "It's the old Hotel Montezuma. It used to sit on the bank of the river just below the bridge into Montezuma. Mostly rivermen used to stop there. According to Mr. Satterly, they used to haul whiskey, lumber, and grain to market down the river.

"But in a huge flood back in the 1850s, the hotel was washed right into the river where it broke apart and was

117

carried downstream. I read that they found pieces of it float-ing all the way down in the Gulf of Mexico."

"Then it can't be real," Clifford whispered, his adam's apple bobbing up and down.

"Sure looks real to me," Mary Ethel said, wringing her hands.

"It must be supernatural," Rosie said as the four of them stared in terror at the dripping shell of the old hotel, its win-dows little more than black sockets, as the building rocked ominously in the water. "But why is it here?"

Hank frowned. "I think it's haunted."

"Haunted?" Clifford quavered.

Hank nodded. "I read about it in an old newspaper ar-ticle at the historical museum. Seems like the old lady that ran the hotel—the Widow Jarling, I think she was called—had an ugly temper. She must have been an unhappy wom-an and she took it out on her guests, always accusing them of being rude and trying to cheat her.

"Worst of all, she abused her hired girl. Now what was her name? Shoot, I just read about it. Martha! That's it, I think. Well, in the article, it said that the Widow Jarling would slap her hired girl across the face—right in front of the guests, who were mostly boatmen moving the barges down the riv-er. She was always finding fault with the girl, yelling at her at the supper table that she wasn't serving people right, and things like that. She worked the girl like a slave, and even took to locking her in the pantry to discipline her."

"Why was she so mean to her?" Rosie asked.

Hank shrugged. "Nobody knows. I do know that young Martha was the only one who didn't escape the hotel that night it was washed away."

118

Suddenly the soprano voice of a young girl called from deep within the hotel, "Help me! I'm drowning. Please help me!"

"Let's get out of here," Clifford cried.

Frantically, Hank tried to paddle them away from the old hotel.

"We're not getting anywhere!" Mary Ethel cried. Despite Hank's best efforts, the boat was being drawn closer to the looming hotel. Thin, floating, as if it were coming from a great distance, the voice continued to beg, "Help me! I'm drowning."

Softly, the nose of the rowboat bumped against the porch steps.

"It's got us under a spell," Clifford cried. "We're all gonna die! I just know it!" Even as he spoke, water began to seep into Clifford's boat at every seam, and all four teenagers were forced against their instincts to jump out onto the porch of the hotel. "My boat!" Clifford moaned, as water overtook the little blue rowboat and it disappeared without a trace beneath the surface.

"Forget the boat!" Hank advised. "We've got to—"

Suddenly he was struck dumb as the vague form of an ancient woman materialized in the doorway. With hair drawn back severely, her gray eyes like splinters of metal, she scowled at him. A heavy-set woman in a calico dress, she grasped a meat cleaver in her right hand, its blade gleaming silver in the light of the moon.

"What do you want?" she snarled. The four of them were too stricken to answer her. "Have you come for a room? Is that what you want? Well, I don't have any vacancies, unless you want a room for the dead."

119

Clifford gulped. "No thanks. We just drifted in here by mistake. But if it's all right with you, we'll be on our way now."

"You're not going anywhere," she said, her voice low and ominous.

"We'll have to swim for it," Hank advised his three companions.

The old lady, presumably the Widow Jarling, laughed as she informed him, "You're completely surrounded by water."

"We can't be that far from the bank," Hank asserted.

"You'll be sucked into the depths," the old woman told him smugly.

Her voice rising again like a violent wind, the girl shrieked, "Help me! I'm drowning!"

"Never mind her," the Widow Jarling snapped furiously. "She's always complaining, that ungrateful child! After all I've done for her! She always had food, clothes, and a roof over her head."

"Help me! I'm drowning!"

"Shut up, Martha!" the old woman shouted.

Steeling himself, Hank asked the old lady, "Where is your hired girl? It sounds like she really needs help. Did you leave her locked up in the pantry during the flood? Is that why she couldn't swim for safety like all the others, including yourself?"

The old lady's blue lips curled. "You're a smart boy, but you'll never see the light of day. Now get inside, all of you!"

"We're not going anywhere," Rosie declared.

The Widow Jarling raised the meat cleaver. "You'll do as I say, unless you want to be chopped into fishbait."

Despite her bulk, she floated across the porch and herded them into the hotel. Slamming the door shut, she cried, "Now there is no escape for you!"

"What are you going to do to us?" Clifford whimpered.

"Nothing!" the old lady declared. "That's the beauty of it. I don't have to do a single thing!"

Hank noticed the water seeping in at the bottom of the door.

"The hotel is sinking back into the river!" Rosie cried.

"That's right," the widow cackled. "Back into the depths—which is where you will spend the rest of eternity, with me and Martha."

Hank had been wondering why the hotel was still intact and why the Widow Jarling remained its mistress. He recalled the newspaper article saying that she had disappeared shortly after the tragedy, never to be seen or heard from again. What was she doing back here in the old hotel? Perhaps Martha had the answer, but how could he ask her without the widow interfering?

The water had already risen to their knees. Remembering that the widow had frequently complained about the rude manners of her guests, Hank thought fast. In a booming voice, he announced, "We're hungry!"

"Hungry?" the Widow Jarling asked, cocking an eye at him.

"Yes! Aren't we, Clifford?"

"What?" Clifford asked, his jaw hung open.

"We want dinner!" Hank demanded.

"But you're about to die," the widow reminded him.

"Who cares?" Hank roared in a boisterous tone of voice. "We want to eat! This will be our last meal, so get a move on and make it a good one, old lady."

The ghost of the Widow Jarling reddened ever so slightly. "That is no way to address a lady, young man. As you can see quite clearly, I have no one to help me here."

Meanwhile, the ghost of Martha the hired girl began to call again, "Help me. I'm drowning."

"What about your girl?" Hank asked, as the water rose to their waists. "She can get the food!"

"I'll have you to know that she's indisposed at the moment," the widow snapped. "Besides, she's no good."

Clifford whispered to Hank, "In case you haven't noticed, we're about to drown here."

"Play along," Hank whispered back.

Flashing the cleaver over her head, the widow raged, "I have a mind to turn you into mincemeat!"

"We're entitled to a filling meal," Hank reminded her in a most boastful tone of voice.

"I already told you Martha cannot come out. I forbid it!"

"How 'bout these girls then?" Hank asked, nodding toward Rosie and Mary Ethel. "They may as well make themselves useful. They can rustle us up some food." The water was ascending to their chests, so Hank knew that they would have to act quickly. "Rosie! Mary Ethel!" he ordered. "Get us some food! Come on! Jump to it!"

Rosie must have sensed that Hank had a plan, for she waded past him, asking in a whisper, "What should we do?"

Hank wasn't sure what, if anything, might save them. Yet he sensed that, for whatever reason, the captivity of Martha was at the root of this dilemma. "Just let Martha out of the pantry," he whispered.

"What did you say to that girl?" the widow demanded.

Hank roared, "I advise you to keep your mouth shut, old lady!"

122

"Why, you're as rude and ill-mannered as any riverman who ever stayed at my hotel. I'm not so sure that I should even let you remain here."

"Then send us on our way, you sour old hag!" Hank shouted back.

"Why you!" The widow swooped over the rising water, with the meat cleaver flashing silver in the interior of the hotel. "I'll chop you to pieces."

Hank ducked under the water, swam across the room, and resurfaced near the opposite wall. "Here I am, you old witch!"

She flew at him, and again he plunged under water. Meanwhile the girls had waded into the kitchen and located the pantry. Out of the corner of his eye, Hank saw them unbolt the door and swing it open.

"What are you doing?" the widow shrieked as she flew at the girls with the meat cleaver. "She is not to be let out!"

Just as the widow was about to bring the cleaver down on Rosie, her attention was diverted by the vague form of a pretty, yet haggard girl which flowed out of the pantry. She had bright orange hair and freckles to match, while the rest of her misty form, including her calico dress and yellow apron, had faded to pastels.

"Get back in there!" yelled the Widow Jarling, wrestling with the girl.

"You can't make me!" Martha answered.

"Yes, I can! I'm your master!"

"I'm beyond your powers now. I've been dead for over a hundred years, and now I'm free of you and your awful hotel!"

With a smile, Martha floated across the space between the still-rising water and the high ceiling, twirling, pivoting, and then vanishing out the transom window over the door. So, Hank realized the truth—the hotel had to remain intact until the ghost of Martha the hired girl was released.

"Now see what you've done!" the widow raged at Hank, going after him with the cleaver again. Suddenly, the hotel shuddered and pitched. Then, it began to break apart.

"My hotel!" the old widow wailed. "It's being destroyed."

"It's long overdue, ma'm," the voice of Martha the hired girl called from the very air.

"Where do you think you're going?" the widow demanded.

"As far away from you as possible, where at last I can rest in peace."

"What about me? I'm just a poor widow and I'll be all alone."

"You've always been alone, ma'm. And you know as well as I do that you're no poor widow. Your husband left you because you were forever nagging at him. Now go back to your grave at the bottom of the river."

"I drowned myself for you, Martha. I was in such deep sorrow over you," the Widow Jarling called to the air.

A bitter laugh rang through the empty shell of the hotel. Martha's voice declared, "No, you didn't, ma'm. You killed yourself in mourning over your precious hotel. This hotel was the only thing you ever truly loved. But you know, ma'm, it was as much a prison for you as it was for me."

"Come back, Martha! Please! I'll be helpless without you! Have pity on me!"

"Goodbye, ma'm. Goodbye, forever!"

An astounding silence gripped the old Hotel Montezuma, then the Widow Jarling turned to Hank and, jabbing a gnarled finger at him, proclaimed, "This is all your fault! If you hadn't come here . . ." She swept after him with the cleaver again, screaming, "I'll kill you, every one of you!"

Hank ducked under the water, just as the entire framework of the building shattered. Submerged, he was spun in a violent whirlpool, not knowing what had happened to his friends, or if they'd all be sucked down forever into the muddy depths of the Wabash River.

He fought against the turbulence, his lungs burning with the desperate need for oxygen. Kicking upward, upward, he at last broke the surface and gasped for air.

Like a great shipwreck, the hotel had become broken pieces of flotsam. Briefly, he glimpsed the white face of the Widow Jarling descending into the depths of the black water. Arms and legs flailing, her face stretched into a silent scream and, as bubbles issued from her throat, she was drawn steadily downward, back to her lonely grave beneath the muddy floor of the Wabash River.

In the stiffening current, Hank was pulled downward himself. Grabbing a splintered timber, he tread water and glanced around for his friends.

Out of the gloom, their heads barely above water, he spotted two figures paddling toward him, and was delighted to recognize Rosie and Mary Ethel clinging to a large timber.

"Where's Clifford?" he asked.

"I haven't seen him," answered Rosie, "not since we went into the kitchen to free Martha."

Mary Ethel was numb. "He must have drowned."

125

Hank was about to dive for him, when Rosie glanced off into the distance and cried, "There he is!"

Sure enough, well out in front of them, squatting in an old wooden washtub, Clifford was paddling furiously toward the bank with a splintered length of floorboard.

"The bank!" Hank cried.

The three of them quickly swam to safety, using the timbers for floatation. As they dragged themselves onto the bank and sagged down next to Clifford, Hank had never been so relieved to set foot on solid ground. Clifford was in such shock that he was just staring straight ahead.

"Some boat ride," Hank muttered.

"I don't think I ever want to go out on that river again," Rosie said.

Mary Ethel frowned. "Not unless it's in a decent boat."

"Clifford?" Hank asked, waving his hand in front of his friend's face.

"Clifford?" Mary Ethel asked.

Finally the boy turned toward her and inquired, "What happened?"

"Don't you remember?" Mary Ethel asked, putting her hand on his forehead.

"He must have blocked it all out," said Rosie.

"Let's get him home," suggested Hank. "There will be plenty of time to fill him in on the details." Anxious to get out of there, they set off walking slowly upriver in the general direction of Boggsville.

"Where's my rowboat?" Clifford demanded. "If you sank it, you're gonna have to pay me for it. It was a beauty. Cost me a fortune, practically."

The Ghost
of Sugar Creek

Nobody knew of the old Manley Settlement, it seemed, except those folks who lived in the immediate vicinity. The blacktop went right by the village, practically, but there was no sign indicating the turnoff, and a thick woods stood between the highway and the valley in which the Manley Settlement was situated. Hank had once stumbled upon the road to it, however, and late one July afternoon he brought Rosie there for a picnic.

In his old pickup, he turned onto a gravel road that wound through a patch of woods so dense that the landscape was completely embraced by shade. Then the road dipped steeply, still meandering left and right, toward the valley through which flowed the clear water of Sugar Creek.

"I've always wondered why they call it Sugar Creek," Rosie said as they cruised to the bottom of the valley.

Hank allowed himself a wisp of a smile. "Well, it's definitely a creek. And about its name, well, you'll see." He wasn't much of a poet, but he knew about sweetness and light.

As they emerged from the deep green foliage, they felt as if they were stepping into another time.

On their right was a long covered bridge, faded red in color, standing mostly in shade, with an occasional splash of light coming through the trees. Just before them, straggling along the edge of the creek, was a group of cabins with gray, hand-hewn logs and tan chinking, most of them dating from before the Civil War, as well as a few tumbledown frame houses. Off to their left, as if to balance the striking presence of the covered bridge, was the towering gray hulk of the old Clayton Grist Mill.

Rising up at the very edge of the water, four stories high, with gray clapboard siding, the water-powered mill had once ground kernels of corn, wheat, and other grains into flour. A long silver sheet of water still streamed, as pure as any dream, over the stone dam that extended across the width of Sugar Creek. But the mill wheel was furred with rust, and the many tiers of windows stared back at them like so many sightless eyes.

Hank gazed over the water, its surface a blurry mirror reflecting the woods and the rock formations on the bank, as well as the mill, the covered bridge, and a ragged portion of the August sky.

"I never even knew this place existed," said Rosie. "It's so lovely, but it looks abandoned."

"Yes," Hank agreed. "And you're right. Nobody lives here anymore."

"Not a single person?"

Hank shook his head.

"I wonder why," Rosie pondered. "It's so pretty here with the river and everything."

"Some folks say the place is haunted, because of the old grist mill."

"Haunted?"

"It seems that everyone who lives here falls victim to misfortune," Hank explained. "A few years ago a man sold his farm to buy the grist mill, but then he up and disappeared."

"What do you mean?"

"It seems that old John Clayton—who built and ran the mill about a hundred years ago—has put a curse on this place."

"You've got to tell me the whole story," Rosie insisted as they drove slowly over the covered bridge, the planks rumbling under the tires of the pickup.

"Let's get settled first," Hank suggested. "I'm starved!"

"I thought you already had some lunch."

"That was practically two hours ago."

Hank parked in an old farm lane just across the river from the mill. "Come on," he said. "I know a nice spot right down here by the water." He retrieved their picnic basket from the back end of the pickup, and they followed a path through the woods to a sandbar which extended from the bank.

Spreading out the blanket, they arranged fried chicken, potato salad, bread and butter pickles, and rhubarb pie, along with a jug of iced tea. Settling down in the cool shade, the water gurgling past, they had a perfect view of the river, the covered bridge, the collection of cabins, and the old grist mill.

Hank would never have come back here at night, but it was lovely during the day, even if it was getting a little late in the afternoon. As they ate their picnic lunch, he related the story of the Clayton Grist Mill, as told to him by old Mr. Satterly.

"The way I heard it, John Clayton was very successful. He produced such an abundance of flour that he couldn't help but get rich. The only problem was he wouldn't allow anyone else to do the same. He had the only mill for miles around, so folks who sold their grain to him always got paid the lowest prices. He also charged way too much if they wanted to have their grain milled. They say he took a gleeful pleasure in the control he had over local folks.

"He prized all of his possessions—his grist mill, his money, even his wife and his children. He jealously guarded them like he did all his property. He made sure they were taken care of and he was always providing for their future. Yet he was so busy that he hardly paid any attention to his children, even when they played around the river and in the mill—which had a lot of moving parts.

"Well, the way Jarvis Satterly tells it, one day Clayton's youngest daughter, Amy, was playing in the mill, in a shaft of light directly behind her father. She was about five years old and by far his favorite. Well, not knowing she was there, he turned around and accidentally bumped her right out the door and onto the great turning mill wheel. She was carried into the water and under the wheel.

"Clayton just stood there, in shock. Luckily, a husky farmer by the name of Luke Riles had come by. He stood there a second, amazed that Clayton wasn't doing anything to save his child. Then, without giving it a second thought, Riles dove into that churning water. He went under for the longest time, while Clayton stood there like he was nailed to the floor. His wife, who sometimes helped out at the mill, rushed over to see what all the commotion was about. She stood there, pulling at her hair, along with their other

130

daughters, and some folks from town hurried over. They were giving up hope when Luke's head blasted up out of the water. He gasped for breath, but he was alive and in his arms he held the small limp body of Amy Clayton.

"The little girl lay there on the bank like a soaking wet rag doll. Luke Riles threw her over on her stomach and pressed with the palms of his hands on her back. But she just lay there. 'Do something!' Mrs. Clayton screamed at her husband, but the gaunt man just stood there, stunned. Riles continued to work furiously over the little girl, who finally issued a small burp. Then her entire body convulsed, and she threw up practically a gallon of water. But the color was returning to her cheeks. She was alive and pretty much fully recovered.

"It seems that Riles had fetched her just as she was being sucked under the mill wheel, tearing her dress free from one of the paddles. He had caught his own leg under the wheel and had the darndest time getting free himself. He kind of twisted his leg up in the rescue, and they say he walked with a limp for the rest of his days, although no one heard him ever complain of it, not once.

"Well, Amy was soggy and frightened, but like I said she lived, thanks to Luke Riles. Now you'd think old Clayton would have thanked Riles, which he did, with a few stiff words, squinting up at the farmer and taking the measure of him with his black eyes. I'm sure he was glad to have his Amy returned to him, but I'm also certain that he resented being obliged to anyone. It was usually other folks who owed him something, not the other way around. Added to that, he had not had the wherewithal himself to do anything to save his daughter.

"Talk went around that Clayton was so cheap and mean that he couldn't, with any sincerity, so much as thank a man for saving the life of his beloved daughter. People were shocked about it, but like most things, the novelty wore off after a while, and it was just something that folks kept in the backs of their minds.

"Things went on pretty much as usual after that—Clayton paying his customers the lowest prices for their grain, since he didn't have any competition. They had no choice but to accept what he paid, unless they drove their wagons the twenty extra miles to the mill in Myrtleville. If they did, after subtracting the cost of the trip, they'd lost whatever they'd gained in getting a higher price.

"One by one, farmers just couldn't make it, and they had to give up and move on. No one was willing to buy their farms so they just abandoned them. Finally, to show you that there is some justice in the world, Clayton's business also fell off—something he apparently hadn't thought much about. You see, it got so bad that he had hardly any grain coming in.

"But to the very end, he never changed his ways. If he had only offered a fair price for the grain, farmers could have survived, and he could still have made a respectable living himself. But it was just too much against his nature for him to think of anyone other than himself.

"Finally, Luke Riles, the farmer who'd rescued his daughter, went bust, which didn't appear to disturb Clayton in the least. In fact, old Clayton appeared relieved to be rid of Riles, who moved away—over to Illinois, I think. Well, that upset folks so much that they finally got together and opened their own mill over in Hillsburg. After that,

Clayton had no grain coming in at all, and it wasn't long before he had to shut down the mill altogether. Folks said you could hear him rant and rave every night. Of course, in his twisted way of thinking, he blamed everyone but himself for the failure of his business—especially Luke Riles.

"Then you know what happened? His daughter, Amy, who was grown by now, eloped with a young farmer. There are some people who say it was the son of Luke Riles who came back for her, but nobody seems to know for certain. Anyway, that really set old Clayton off, because she was his favorite.

"He went so crazy that his wife and the other two daughters also ran off on him, taking all the bags of money he had hoarded, and old Clayton ended up his life with absolutely nothing. And it was all because he was so greedy in the first place.

"More and more he focused the blame for his failure on Luke Riles. In his mind, he figured that if Riles hadn't saved his daughter, no one would have had any sympathy for the farmer, and they never would have set up their own mill. Then, one day, John Clayton suddenly vanished himself. People suspected that he was so ashamed of himself that he had slunk off in the dead of night. Nobody knew where he had gone, and since the mill was closed up tight, no one happened to go inside for the longest time. But as the years passed, folks began to hear a howling inside the mill and a voice crying out into the night, 'I curse you and all your descendants! This village is cursed!'

"Thinking that old Clayton had returned to the mill, or that he might be still holed up there after all those years, people got pretty scared. They called the sheriff, who had to use a wrecking bar to pry open one of the heavy doors. When he'd left, Clayton had bolted all the doors and shuttered all the first floor windows. Well, the sheriff explored the building, floor by floor, not finding anything out of the ordinary. Then he climbed the steps to the highest floor, and there he found the skeleton of John Clayton dangling by the neck from a rafter.

"Clayton hadn't run off at all. He'd hanged himself many years ago. His body had completely decomposed so that nothing was left except for his bones, and the blue work clothes hanging on them, still dusted with flour. Well, the sheriff was real disturbed by the skeleton, but it being his duty, he went and cut it down, knowing he would have to carry it to the undertaker's and arrange for a proper burial.

"He opened his pocket knife, reached up, and sliced through the rope, intending to catch the bundle of dusty old bones as it fell to the floor. But, the moment he cut the rope, the ghost of John Clayton sprang forth, with a huge grin on its face. It chased the sheriff around the storeroom, and when it caught him, the ghost flung him head first from the fourth floor window.

"The sheriff landed on the mill wheel, breaking his neck and just about every other bone in his body. He died a week later. Since then nobody's dared go back into that mill and the ghost of John Clayton has run wild—for the past hundred or so years. Every night he calls out, 'I curse you and all your descendants. I place a curse on this village.' I don't know if the curse is real, but the ghost sure is. Folks didn't like living near a haunted mill, and they gradually moved away. That's why the village is abandoned and no new people have wanted to settle here."

Throughout the story, Rosie had been listening intently. At its conclusion she asked, "But can it really be true, Hank? It's hard to believe that there's a ghost running loose in that grist mill right across the creek. It's so peaceful and pretty here."

"I don't think he still calls out into the night, since no one lives here anymore," Hank explained. "But he's still there, all right. Over the years kids have explored the old mill at night."

"Did they find anything?" Rosie asked.

Hank swallowed. "Two of them got caught in the old wooden gears of the mill and were ground up like flour. It could have been an accident, but if it was, why were the gears moving? And another boy was found floating downstream of the mill, facedown in the water."

Hank had taken so long with the story that dusk was settling like a veil over them. "I didn't mean for us to be out here this late," he said. "Maybe we ought to clear out before the ghost catches sight of us."

"I guess so," Rosie said reluctantly.

Hank sighed. "What's the matter, Rosie? You're not curious about that old mill, are you?"

"Well, wouldn't you like to see if there really is a ghost?"

"I suppose so, but I'm not curious enough to get us killed."

Rosie reasoned, "If we stayed here on the sandbar, it couldn't get us, could it? We're all the way across the water. As long as we're not inside the mill we won't be in danger. The ghost never leaves the grist mill, does it?"

"I don't know. I suppose not," Hank admitted.

Rosie snuggled closer to him. "Besides, it's such a pretty night."

Hank didn't like the idea at all. But having run out of arguments, he sighed, "Well, okay. But we're not going anywhere near that mill."

Her excitement rising, Rosie noted, "There are so many windows, and we've got such a good view, we're bound to see the ghost of John Clayton. That is, if it comes out."

Gradually the night deepened around them. There was the gurgle of Sugar Creek, the wind sifting through the trees which overhung the bank, and the occasional groan of the covered bridge.

"What was that?" Rosie whispered, clutching Hank's arm.

"I didn't hear anything."

"Well, I did!"

Presently a raccoon crept along the edge of the water, sifting for crawdads with its delicate front paws. They watched as it worked its way past them.

In forlorn silence the mill stood against the heat of that August night.

Finally Hank suggested, "It's late. Maybe we'd better—"

"Wait!" Rosie whispered, gripping Hank's arm tightly.

A pale light flickered from the farthest left window on the top floor of the grist mill. Then another light and another went on, until the mill was faintly lit up against the night sky. In a steady downward sequence, lights began to shine in each of the windows on the lower floors, until the entire mill was ablaze with light.

"There's someone in there!" Rosie said, excitement rising in her voice.

Hank had no interest in finding out who it might be, yet he found his attention drawn toward the old grist mill.

"How can there be lights when there's no electricity?" Rosie asked.

"They could be candles," Hank observed. "Maybe we ought to get out of here."

Just then Hank glimpsed a movement in the window. It was some distance from them, but he could distinctly make out a ghostly form in old denim work clothes—with a length of rope around its neck.

"John Clayton," he whispered.

Rosie gasped, "He's looking right at us!"

"He can't see us," Hank argued. "We're sitting in the dark."

"I don't know about that," Rosie muttered. "He seems to be staring right at us. I'm scared."

Presently the ghost dissolved back into the interior of the mill.

For several minutes, Hank and Rosie looked for it to reappear, but with no success. "Let's leave while we've got a chance," Hank suggested. "That ghost could be anywhere around here." Snatching up the picnic basket, they headed up the bank, just as a twig snapped.

"What was that?" Rosie asked breathlessly.

"Let's not wait to find out," Hank said, and the two of them plunged ahead through the night-blackened foliage—just as the ghost of John Clayton stepped across the path.

"I've been looking for you, Amy," he said, his teeth of a sickening yellow color clenched into a permanent grin.

"I'm not Amy!" Rosie gasped.

The ghost of John Clayton sneered, "Maybe not, but you'll do. I need someone to keep me company." He reached out to grab her.

"Out of our way!" Hank commanded, stepping forward to protect Rosie. With a violent slap of his hand, the ghost sent him flying backward several yards through the air, directly into Sugar Creek. Then, throwing Rosie over his shoulder, the ghost sprang down the path which wound along the bank of the creek.

Fighting against the current, Hank grabbed a snag and managed to swim back to the sandbar. Through the foliage, silhouetted in the light of the young moon, he caught glimpses of Rosie and the ghost moving toward the dam, and he raced after them.

With Rosie slung over his shoulder, the ghost deftly climbed across an abutment of moss-covered rocks by the waterfall, and edged out across the dam. Hank followed, carefully balancing himself on the slippery stone ledge, between the relatively calm pool to his right and the cascading waterfall to his left. The water going over the dam was just ankle-deep, but it exerted a tremendous pull, and the dam was covered with slippery algae, threatening to yank him over the waterfall and into the rocks below.

Having succeeded in crossing the dam, the ghost slipped into the mill with Rosie still flung over his shoulder. "Help!" she cried. "Please help me, Hank!"

When Hank reached the other side, he discovered that the ghost had bolted the thick plank door shut. All of the windows of the first floor were tightly shuttered with hand-sawn planks from the previous century.

"I have you now!" the ghost shrieked from inside the grist mill. "My dear girl, you have finally returned to me!"

"But I'm not Amy," Rosie pleaded.

"Then you shall replace her!" the ghost replied. "These long years I've been waiting for a pretty young girl to hap-

139

pen by, but there have only been boys—until now. And now that you're here, I'll keep you with me for all eternity."

"No, I won't. Hank will rescue me. You'll see."

"What can he do? He is just a boy. He is no match for my powers."

At the moment Hank was not even able to find a way into the mill. He searched around the stone foundation, but it was well constructed, and the entire mill appeared to be as solid as any prison. Returning to the platform overlooking the mill wheel and the river, he surveyed the upper windows.

Through one window, he could see that the ghost had brought Rosie to a second floor room where he tied her arms behind her back. Standing her on a chair, the ghost placed a rope around her neck, and knotted the other end securely to a rafter. He said, "Don't be frightened. Death will come quickly to you, my Amy. You'll see I am a kind man after all."

Rosie struggled futilely to free herself.

There was no way to climb to the upper window and Hank searched frantically for an entrance to the mill. He was at a complete loss, until he noticed the great turning mill wheel. If he could jump onto it, it would carry him upward, and he could spring into the window. Of course, if he failed, he would be carried under the creaking wheel and surely drowned, if not first crushed to death.

Edging back out onto the dam so that he would have a good angle, he flung himself onto the wheel, barely catching one of the slippery paddles. The wheel swiftly arced upward and, at the highest point, Hank jumped for the window—at least he tried to, but he had caught his belt on a splintered paddle.

Abruptly, he was thrust over the top and downward into the churning water and swept under the wheel. His back scraped on the creek bottom, and he was certain that he would be crushed to death between the wheel and the bottom of the river. Having no choice, he hung on, barely squeezing through the narrow gap, and was again carried upward where he gasped for air.

At least he wasn't crushed, but he was badly scraped up. Seconds later, still caught, he was thrust under the water again. He struggled desperately to free his belt buckle from the wheel. On the third trip around, he had gotten the belt unstuck and, on the fourth trip, he sprang for the window, barely catching the sill with his fingertips.

"What was that?" the ghost cried.

He kicked the chair out from under Rosie who dropped suddenly, the rope tightening around her neck. Her feet kicked wildly.

"No!" Hank screamed, scrambling over the sill and rushing toward her.

The ghost whirled on him, but Hank had opened his pocket knife, and with a running leap he slashed at the rope from which Rosie dangled. Like a deadweight, she dropped to the floor.

Throwing a lever, Clayton set an array of wooden gears into operation. Then he charged after Hank. Around and around the mill they raced, Hank barely dodging the ghost. He slashed back at the ghost with his pocket knife, but only managed to shred his work clothes.

Hank knew that he would not be able to elude the ghost for long. As he veered this way and that around the thick beams and machinery, he noticed the skeleton of John Clayton still lying in a corner, forgotten, probably where the sheriff had dropped it many years ago. An idea came to Hank. As he ran, he tried to study the workings of the mill. He couldn't begin to understand most of the equipment, with a vast assortment of gears and canvas belts which set the mill into motion—at least not with a ghost pursuing him. However, Hank did note the large, flat millstone which ground the grain after it passed down a chute.

He got an idea, just as the ghost was closing the distance between them.

"Wait!" he gasped. "I give up!"

"What?" the ghost demanded.

"Yes!" Hank cried. "I can't win against you. I'll work for you. For free."

"For free?" the ghost asked eagerly.

"You can't get a better bargain," Hank pointed out.

The ghost fixed its misty eyes on the young man. "What's the catch?"

"Since you're going to kill me anyway, at least let me stay here with you and Rosie. If you teach me how, I'll operate the mill for you."

The ghost remained suspicious. "Wait a minute. I don't need help. There's no grain coming in."

"Well, I can at least light the candles at night, and I can help you to scare away intruders. All you have to do is show me how the mill works," Hank said, stepping dangerously close to the chute.

"Most certainly," said the ghost of John Clayton, that evil grin fixed upon his face. He eased next to Hank, his airy arm brushing against Hank's shirt sleeve.

Seizing the opportunity, the ghost lunged at Hank, attempting to knock the young man into the gaping mouth of the grain chute. But Hank had suspected that the ghost could not be trusted. Anticipating the attack, Hank stepped aside and instead rushed to the skeleton, lying in the dusty corner, which he quickly flung down the chute.

"Nooooo!" the ghost shrieked. As the skeleton clattered down the chute to the millstone, its bones broke apart. One by one, as the flat millstone rotated, the bones were splintered, crushed, and ground to a fine white powder. Bouncing against the millstone, the skull was the last part of John Clayton's skeleton to be pulverized.

As Hank had suspected, the ghost of John Clayton also vanished. He rushed to Rosie, hoping against hope that she was not dead. Loosening the rope from around her neck, he held her in his arms. She had a nasty red burn at her throat, but she was breathing ever so softly. Holding her close, Hank spoke softly, "Rosie. Dear Rosie."

Her eyes fluttered open. "Hank? Is that you?" Anxious to vacate the premises, she said, "I wish we'd never come here."

"Wait," Hank said.

Descending to the lower level of the mill, they found that the bones of John Clayton had indeed been ground to a fine powder which, along with the fibers of the rope hung around his neck, had been deposited into the flour bin. "I wanted to make sure he's gone forever," Hank said as they gazed upon the dust that was once John Clayton.

The two young people were shocked by their harrowing experience, but also pleased to have at last freed that lovely place of an evil spirit. Before they departed, Hank disengaged the machinery and, walking from floor to floor, they blew out every candle in the mill.

THE END

Afterword

Have you ever wondered if there are ghosts roaming deep in the past of your family, neighborhood, town, or the surrounding countryside?

You probably don't want to actually explore any of their haunts, like Hank and his friend Clifford who found themselves up to their eyeballs in dangerous situations. However, if you'd like to scare up a few good ghost stories yourself, start by asking your parents and grandparents. They may know some interesting family stories. Or perhaps they can tell you about another relative—a great uncle, an elderly aunt, or a distant cousin—who has a story or two to share with you.

You can also ask your teacher and school librarian. Have they heard any good stories about the history of the people and places in your community?

For your next step, plan a visit to your public library, local museum, or historical society, as well as the offices of your hometown newspaper. The people who work in these places tend to be very knowledgeable about local history and they can usually tell you plenty of stories about the past—especially if they have lived in the area for many years. More than likely, they'll also be glad to help you discover fascinating books, old photographs, newspaper clippings, letters, and other documents to help you in your research as a ghost detective.

Like the tales in *The Fresh Grave*, the stories you find may be completely fictional—but there's always a good lesson or two and lots of thrills in a spooky yarn. Or the stories you unearth may be absolutely true. Sometimes, nobody may know for certain whether they're true or not. Whatever the case, collecting stories is a fascinating way to learn how people really lived in the past. So—happy ghost hunting!

About the Author

R aymond Bial has published over thirty critically-acclaimed books as a writer and photographer. His popular photo-essay books for children celebrating American history and heritage are appreciated as "crossover books" that appeal to both younger readers and adults. These titles are especially delightful for parents, grandparents, teachers, and librarians to share with children.

The Fresh Grave is the author's first work of fiction. He claims he is personally very much afraid of ghosts, and the stories were written for his daughter Anna who loves scary stories. Although the stories are pure fiction, Raymond drew upon his own childhood years growing up on farms and in small towns to create realistic and believable settings. The stories were originally read to Anna on the family's back porch in the evenings—much as Raymond's grandfather, rocking back and forth on a porch swing, had once told ghost stories to Raymond's mother when she was a child.

The director of a small college library, Raymond Bial lives with his wife Linda and three children, Anna, Sarah, and Luke, in a reasonably quiet little town in the Midwest.

Other Children's Books by Raymond Bial
Amish Home
Cajun Home
Corn Belt Harvest
County Fair
Frontier Home
Mist Over the Mountains: Appalachia and Its People
Portrait of a Farm Family
Shaker Home
The Strength of These Arms: Life in the Slave Quarters
The Underground Railroad
Where Lincoln Walked
With Needle and Thread: A Book About Quilts